Other Books by Harriet Steel

Becoming Lola

Salvation

City of Dreams

Following the Dream

The Inspector de Silva Mysteries:

Trouble in Nuala

AN INSPECTOR DE SILVA MYSTERY

DARK CLOUDS OVER NUALA

HARRIET STEEL

Author's Note

Welcome to the second book in my Inspector de Silva mystery series. Like the first one, this is a self-contained story and I have done my best to write it so that readers who are new to the series will not feel they are missing out on anything. As a reader myself, however, I usually find that my enjoyment of the characters in a series is deepened by reading the books in order. With that in mind, I have included thumbnail sketches of those who took a major part in *Trouble in Nuala* and reprinted the book's introduction, with apologies to those who have already read it.

Two years ago, I had the great good fortune to visit the island of Sri Lanka, the former Ceylon. I fell in love with the country straight away, awed by its tremendous natural beauty and the charm and friendliness of its people who seem to have recovered extraordinarily well from the tragic civil war between the two main ethnic groups, the Sinhalese and the Tamils. I had been planning to write a new detective series for some time and when I came home, I decided to set it in Ceylon in the 1930s, a time when British Colonial rule created interesting contrasts, and sometimes conflicts, with traditional culture. Thus, Inspector Shanti de Silva and his friends were born.

My thanks go to my editor, John Hudspith, for all the excellent work he has done on *Dark Clouds Over Nuala*, and to Jane Dixon Smith for designing the layout and a cover that fulfilled all my dreams. As always too, I am extremely grateful to my husband, Roger, and my daughter, Ellie, for their encouragement and support. Any mistakes are my own. If any characters resemble persons living or dead, this is purely coincidental. The town of Nuala is also fictitious.

Some pre-publication readers mentioned that an explanation of a few unfamiliar culinary terms would be helpful. I hope the following are of use:

A hopper: a kind of crispy pancake cooked in a bowl shape. It's usually served at breakfast with egg or curry in it.

String hoppers: noodles.

Brinjal: a special curry dish made from eggplant (aubergine).

Note on languages.

The languages of Sri Lanka are Sinhalese, Tamil and English. An educated man like de Silva would speak all three.

**Characters who appear regularly
in the Inspector de Silva Mysteries**

Inspector Shanti de Silva. He began his police career in
Ceylon's capital city, Colombo, but, in middle age, he married and accepted a promotion to inspector in charge of the
small force in the hill town of Nuala. Likes: a quiet life with
his beloved wife; his car; good food; his garden. Dislikes:
interference in his work by his British masters; formal oc-
casions. Race and religion: Sinhalese, Buddhist.

Sergeant Prasanna. In his mid-twenties and starting to
find his feet in his job. Likes: cricket (and is exceptionally
good at it). Dislikes: his mother trying to marry him off.
Race and religion: Sinhalese, Buddhist.

Constable Nadar. A few years younger than Prasanna and
less confident. Married with a baby boy. Likes: his food;
making toys for his baby son. Dislikes: sleepless nights.
Race and religion: Tamil, Hindu.

The British:

Jane de Silva. She came to Ceylon as a governess to a
wealthy colonial family and met and married de Silva a few
years later. A no-nonsense lady with a dry sense of humour.
Likes: detective novels; cinema and dancing. Dislikes:
snobbishness.

Archie Clutterbuck. Assistant government agent in Nuala
and as such, responsible for administration and keeping law

and order in the area. Likes: his Labrador, Darcy; fishing; hunting big game. Dislikes: being argued with; the heat.

Florence Clutterbuck. Archie's wife, a stout, forthright lady. Likes: being queen bee; organising other people. Dislikes: people who don't defer to her at all times.

William Petrie. Government agent for the Central Province and therefore Archie Clutterbuck's boss. A charming exterior hides a steely character. Likes: getting things done. Dislikes: inefficiency.

Lady Caroline Petrie. William's wife and, as the daughter of the 13th Earl of Axford, a titled lady in her own right. A gentle, elegant woman. Likes: making other people feel at ease. Dislikes: things not being done properly; lack of consideration for others.

Doctor David Hebden. Doctor for the Nuala area. He travelled widely before fetching up in Nuala. Unmarried and, under his professional shell, rather shy. Likes: cricket. Dislikes: formality.

CHAPTER 1

New Year's Eve 1933
Western Australia

As the minutes to midnight ticked away, ever greater numbers of revellers crowded into the noisy bar. The dark-haired man limped back to his table with a glass of beer in his hand. Halfway there, someone knocked into him and he stumbled, lurching into a burly miner and slopping some of the beer down the fellow's jacket. As the miner jerked round, he waited for a blow but, to his relief, all that came was a gust of hot, whisky breath and a muttered curse.

The young man waiting for him at the table was still on his own. 'They aren't coming,' he said miserably. He raked one hand through his fair hair. His forehead glistened and his skin had a greenish hue.

What was there to say? It was impossible to put things right.

Morosely, the young man reached for the bottle of whisky on the table and poured a shot into a glass. He drained the whisky in one gulp and reached for the bottle again, but the dark-haired man pushed it out of his reach.

'Enough. We're getting out of here.'

Glowering, the young man tried to get to his feet but staggered; the table rocked as he grabbed the edge. The whisky bottle and the glasses slid off, smashing on the stone floor. He stared bleakly at the jagged pieces glinting in the puddle of whisky and beer then almost toppled into the lap of the heavily rouged and powdered woman sitting at the next table. He clutched at her dress to steady himself, dislodging the neckline.

'You'll have to pay if you want to look down there, sweetheart.' She laughed and shoved him off, rearranging her cleavage.

Her scowling companion started from his seat. He wore an open-necked shirt that revealed a burly chest. The sinews in his thick neck bulged and he clenched his fists.

The dark-haired man pulled a couple of dollars out of his pocket and pushed them across the table. 'Sorry about my friend. He's had a few too many tonight, and some bad news. Please, have a drink on us. Happy New Year.'

The woman's companion hesitated then shrugged and sat down again. 'Happy New Year, friend. No hard feelings. But I'd get yer mate out of here before someone rearranges that pretty face of his.'

'Thanks for the advice,' the dark-haired man said dryly.

Outside, the temperature had markedly dropped. The young man gagged and doubled over. His companion helped him to the side of the road and looked away as he vomited bile and alcohol. When it was over, he handed the young man a handkerchief. 'Here, use this.'

The streets grew quieter as they neared the hotel. In the lobby, the woman behind the desk glared at them. 'I hope there's going to be no extra laundry. I charge double, New Year's Eve or not.'

After making a stumbling ascent of the stairs, they reached a narrow landing, painted a drab shade of brown, that presented a series of doors. They stopped at the last one; it was unlocked. Inside was a pokey room. A lightbulb with a cheap paper shade – the graveyard of years of dead flies – cast a glaucous light over an ugly table and chair and a bed covered with a faded red counterpane. The young man crumpled onto it and turned his face to the wall.

The window was shut so the dark-haired man went over and struggled with the sash. After a few moments, it yielded and air crept into the stuffy room. Distant cheers and shouts drifted from the centre of town. A million shooting stars and fountains of light: red, blue, green, silver and gold, split the night sky. As the first round of fireworks faded, welcoming in 1934, a succession of others took its place, each volley crackling and fizzing before it died, until a pall of smoke lay over the rooftops.

His heart hollow, the dark-haired man went over to the bed and looked down at his companion, who, in spite of the commotion, was asleep. Very gently, he reached out a hand and stroked his cheek then brushed back a lock of hair that had stuck to the pale, clammy skin. After a few moments, he returned to the window to view the display. His clenched fists rested heavily on the windowsill.

Then fear seized him. Was it his imagination or had something deep in the earth moved?

CHAPTER 2

April 1935
Ceylon

It was the day of the Empire Cup, the most fashionable event in Nuala's racing calendar. While he waited for his wife, Jane, to get ready, Inspector Shanti de Silva strolled around his garden. Overnight rain had revived the red earth and freshened the trees and flowers. His beloved roses looked splendid and the grass under his feet was a springy, emerald carpet.

He turned to see Jane walking across the lawn towards him. 'Do I look suitable?'

'Of course you do, you always look lovely. Is that a new dress?'

She shook her head. 'Shanti dear, I've worn it dozens of times.'

'Well, it's very nice.'

'But I have bought something new for the dinner at the Residence tomorrow. I hope you don't mind?'

'As long as we still have money to eat,' he said with a grin.

She pinched his sleeve. 'You know I don't spend extravagant sums on dresses, and this is very pretty - a sea-green silk with a bolero jacket. I think you'll like it. I plan to wear it with my pearls.'

'I'm only teasing, and I'm sure I'll love it.' He offered her his arm. 'Shall we be on our way? It would be a pity to miss the first race.'

The Morris Cowley waited for them on the drive. One of the houseboys had washed and polished its smart navy paintwork and chrome fittings and they gleamed in the sun. De Silva started the engine and the car crunched over Sunnybank's gravelled drive and turned onto the road.

'I've been looking forward to this for weeks,' remarked Jane, putting up one hand to hold her hat in place as they speeded up. Sunshine filtered through the green tunnel of trees above them, dappling the road with light and shade. 'Florence Clutterbuck says William Petrie and Lady Caroline will be here today. They're up from Kandy for a while and have brought Lady Caroline's nephew and his wife with them.'

De Silva didn't comment. The arrival of this nephew, Ralph Wynne-Talbot, and his wife, Helen, seemed to have acted like a stone tossed into the quiet waters of the de Silvas' sleepy little home town. The Wynne-Talbots were being treated as the most exciting visitors to come to Nuala in a long time. He hoped they were not going to disappoint everyone.

At any rate, Florence Clutterbuck, the wife of the assistant government agent, Archie Clutterbuck, and self-appointed leader of Nuala society, clearly intended to make the most of the visit. It wasn't every day that her husband's superior and his wife bestowed their company on Nuala, let alone brought prestigious relatives with them. Among other things, Florence was organising a grand dinner to which everyone who was anyone in Nuala had been invited. De Silva supposed he should be flattered that he and Jane were on the list, although he wasn't fond of having to dress up for the occasion.

Jane sniffed. 'Well, aren't you curious to see them?'

He chuckled. 'If you want me to be, then I am.'

His wife reached across the steering wheel and gave his knuckles a brisk rap. 'You're very provoking.'

De Silva smiled and changed gear as he decelerated to negotiate the bullock cart lumbering towards them. It surprised him that his down-to-earth wife was so excited about the whole business; he concluded it must be an English trait to take such an interest in the British aristocracy, in which the Wynne-Talbots were, apparently, about to play a notable part.

Jane had explained to him several days previously that they were in Ceylon en route from Australia to England. In England they would be visiting Ralph's grandfather, William Wynne-Talbot, 13th Earl of Axford, who was not in the best of health. His death, when it unfortunately occurred, would make Ralph the fourteenth earl and master of a large tract of the English Midlands. He would also inherit Axford Court, generally considered to be one of the finest stately homes in England. In the days of Henry VIII, it had replaced the draughty, medieval castle built by Guillaume de Wynne, a Norman knight who had come over to England with William the Conqueror.

Henry had rewarded Guillaume's Tudor descendant with the earldom for his services to the Crown. The first earl had the good sense to keep his king's favour by building a house that was large and magnificent enough to eclipse those of his peers, but not so grand that it overshadowed the royal palaces.

Yes, Ralph Wynne-Talbot's prospects were bright: a great landowner and a belted earl with the surety of a welcome in the highest echelons of society.

'But one thing puzzles me,' Jane remarked when she had imparted all this information. 'I don't understand why Ralph Wynne-Talbot has no title. Florence Clutterbuck was speculating as to why that should be and, even though I don't like gossip, she does have a point.'

'Why would he have one? I thought you said it was his grandfather who was the Earl of Axford.'

'Yes, but where an ancient family like theirs is concerned, they usually have more than one title. The earldom will be the principal one but any lesser one, say viscount, is usually given to the male heir as a courtesy.'

De Silva shrugged. 'Perhaps there is no lesser one.'

'It would be odd. Florence thinks it strange too that Lady Caroline has never mentioned her nephew up until now. I wouldn't expect to have heard about him but the Clutterbucks have known the Petries for many more years than we have.'

'There's probably some perfectly simple explanation,' said De Silva, rather bored with the topic. 'Nearly there. I hope there are some decent parking places left.'

The course was already bustling with chattering, laughing racegoers. A few had arrived by car but most on foot so, to de Silva's satisfaction, the Morris came to rest in an ideal place close to the entrance to the course.

Racing was a popular sport with all classes of Nuala's society and visitors in saris and sarongs mingled with those wearing floral frocks, western-style suits or even morning dress and top hats. As they passed one of the refreshment tents, de Silva's famously acute nose picked up an appetising aroma of cashew and pea curry. He and Jane had eaten lunch at home, but he must remember where the tent was. He could always find room for his favourite curry.

They made their way to the paddock where the horses entered in the first race were already collected, circling and fidgeting as if they knew that the race was imminent and were keen to be off. Their jockeys, mostly gentleman amateurs looking smart in their shining boots, breeches and colourful silks, chatted to owners and trainers.

'I always think it's most ingenious that they find so many different combinations of colours and patterns,' said

Jane. She pointed to one of the jockeys. 'I like the look of the gold stars on the blue background.'

De Silva glanced at his card and then over at the rails where the bookies had set up their pitches. 'He's riding number twelve, Firefly. The odds are a hundred to eight.'

'Oh dear, not much chance of winning then.'

'You can never tell, although I agree it seems unlikely.'

'Oh, but it's a pretty name, maybe I'll put a few rupees on each way.'

'Well, I suppose a pretty name is as good a reason as any. We'd better get over to the bookies, then. The race will start soon.'

Unfortunately, Firefly finished second to last but the de Silvas' choice in the next race fared better, coming fourth. They were nearing the paddock to see the horses entered in the third race, the Empire Cup itself, when Jane shaded her eyes and pointed to a group standing inside the ring.

'Oh, look over there! The Petries, and Florence and Archie Clutterbuck with them. The young couple must be the Wynne-Talbots. My, but she's lovely, isn't she? What beautiful blonde hair she has, and so slim. He looks very handsome too.'

De Silva studied the young couple without a great deal of interest, but he had to admit that his wife was right: Mrs Wynne-Talbot was a stunner. Tall and slender as a birch sapling, she had hair like spun gold, regular features that would not have been out of place on a Greek statue and delphinium-blue eyes. Her husband was equally striking but in a more robust way with dark-brown, wavy hair, a strong jaw and an athletic build.

Archie Clutterbuck noticed them and beckoned.

'Ah, my love,' whispered de Silva. 'Here's your chance to meet this famous couple.'

'Oh dear, I wish I'd worn something smarter, and whatever shall we say to them?'

'You look extremely smart. And as for what to say to them, there's never a gap in the conversation with Florence Clutterbuck around.'

Jane giggled. 'That's very true.'

'Splendid afternoon, eh?' Archie Clutterbuck boomed genially as the de Silvas joined the little group that had formed around a fine chestnut filly. 'Mrs de Silva! A pleasure to see you.' He turned to the Petries. 'Do you remember Inspector de Silva and his wife?'

'Of course we do,' Lady Caroline said with a smile. 'We often tell people about your triumph in the Renshaw case, Inspector. I hope life has been a little more restful for you recently. But I forget my manners - may I present my nephew, Ralph Wynne-Talbot, and his wife, Helen?'

Helen of Troy, how apt, thought de Silva. He hoped she would stop at being a beauty, and not go on to cause a catastrophe.

They shook hands and exchanged polite murmurings; Helen Wynne-Talbot gave them a fleeting smile. Although she was tall for a woman, her hand was small and delicate and felt as insubstantial as a feather in de Silva's. In contrast, her husband's grip was firm and his smile all-encompassing. To de Silva's way of thinking, however, the charm was just a little too practised.

Jane stroked the chestnut's neck and the filly snorted and nuzzled her hand.

'You're fond of horses, Mrs de Silva?' asked William Petrie.

'Yes, when I was a governess in England, one of the families I worked for were keen riders and had a large stable.'

'We hope this one's in with a chance today. Our trainer tells us she's been performing very well over the gallops. But racing's a funny old game, so I don't suggest you put the family fortune on her.'

Jane smiled. 'Perhaps just a little flutter.'

'Do you have many horses running today, sir?' de Silva asked.

'Only two. Kashmir in the second to last race and this one, Carolina Moon.' He touched Lady Caroline's arm. 'A tribute to my dear wife and a favourite song of ours.'

'And a delightful one, I must say,' said Florence Clutterbuck. De Silva smiled to himself. Florence probably thought she had been left out of the conversation for quite long enough.

A voice boomed over the loudspeaker calling the horses to the starting post. Carolina Moon tossed her head and showed the whites of her eyes. Her groom, a small wiry man, brought her under control and the jockey mounted. As he gathered the reins and made ready to go, they all wished him luck.

The de Silvas said their goodbyes and walked over to one of the bookies. After a brief deliberation, they put a few rupees on Carolina Moon to win then went to find a space at the rails near the finishing post.

It took several minutes for the stewards to marshal the seething mass of horses into some kind of order, then the starter fired his pistol and they were off. The track had softened a little with the rain but the horses' hooves still thundered over the cropped turf as their jockeys crouched low in the saddles, urging them on. Slowly, the field separated into two groups, the leaders ten, then twenty yards ahead of the rest.

'See how her jockey's holding Petrie's filly back in fourth place,' said de Silva. 'He'll let the front runners set the pace then come through to win in the last few furlongs.'

Jane squeezed his arm. 'You're very knowledgeable all of a sudden. I hope that's right.'

'Of course it is. Haven't we had a tip from the horse's mouth?'

'With reservations, dear.' Jane raised an eyebrow.

The noise from the crowd increased as the horses streamed like a multi-coloured river around the final bend and into the home straight. 'What did I tell you? She's moving up!' He struck the rail with his race card.

'I hope the jockey hasn't left it too late.'

The horses bunched so that it was hard to see who was ahead, then by inches Carolina Moon took the lead. In a few moments, she was clear and streaking towards the finishing line. A roar went up as she passed the post.

'What a magnificent performance!' De Silva beamed.

'The Petries will be pleased. I hope we see them to congratulate them. And how nice to have such an exciting result when Lady Caroline's nephew and his wife are with them.'

'We'd better go and collect our winnings.'

'Oh yes, we mustn't forget those.'

'And after that, let's go to one of the refreshment tents and celebrate. I'm beginning to feel a little peckish.'

Jane laughed. 'Alright, I suppose it *is* a special occasion.'

As they left the bookies, they met Archie Clutterbuck who had also been collecting his winnings. 'Don't tell my wife,' he begged. 'Florence doesn't really approve of gambling. I left her with the Petries and told her I needed to speak to someone on official matters for a few minutes.'

They walked back together to where he had left Florence with the Petries and congratulated them on the win.

'Yes, all very gratifying,' William Petrie said when he had thanked them. 'I hope Kashmir continues our run of luck. Now, if you'll excuse us, we must go and congratulate our people.'

Florence lowered her voice conspiratorially as the Petries and the Wynne-Talbots walked away. 'What a charming couple the Petries are and the nephew will be an ornament to the aristocracy, I'm sure. But the wife!' Florence rolled her eyes. 'She's a funny little thing. Nothing to say for herself at all. I can't imagine how she'll manage as chatelaine of a great house like Axford Court. When she becomes Countess of Axford, she'll be expected to take her place in London society *and* take the lead in the county too, when the family's in residence. It will be essential for her to stamp her authority on her staff.'

When he wanted some light relief from his usual reading matter of the English classics, de Silva enjoyed the stories of P G Wodehouse. A vision of Wodehouse's creation, the stately butler, Jeeves, floated into his mind. Florence Clutterbuck had a point. As Jane would say, one would need to get up very early in the morning to stay ahead of Jeeves.

Archie Clutterbuck frowned. 'That's enough, my dear. Given time, I'm sure Mrs Wynne-Talbot will grow used to her duties and discharge them well.'

Florence harrumphed and shot him an icy look. 'I only meant that one can't underestimate what hard work it is fulfilling one's social duties. I can vouch for that myself. The last few days have been so busy with arrangements for tomorrow's dinner.'

'And I'm sure it will be a great success,' her husband added quickly. 'Now, would you ladies like a glass of something? I saw Pimm's on offer in one of the tents.'

'That would be lovely,' said Jane with a smile. Reluctantly, De Silva relinquished his hopes of that cashew and pea curry.

They headed for one of the tents and found a table. Clutterbuck ordered a jug of Pimm's. For a while, they chatted over their drinks then he stood up.

'If the ladies will excuse me, I think I'll go outside for a smoke. Join me, de Silva?'

'Certainly.' He wondered whether there was anything particular Clutterbuck wanted to talk about or whether this was just one of the informal chats he liked to engineer to keep abreast of things in Nuala.

They left Jane to listen to Florence on the subject of the following night's plans and to commiserate over all the work involved and went outside to find a quiet corner. Clutterbuck produced a monogrammed gold cigarette case and offered one to de Silva.

'No thank you, sir.'

'Ah, forgot. You're not a smoker, are you? Good of you to keep me company then.'

'A pleasure, sir. I'm glad of some fresh air.'

'Anything to report?' asked Clutterbuck when he had exhaled the first puff.

'Nothing important, sir. There's been the usual petty pilfering in the bazaar and a few disputes between stallholders but in general things are quiet.'

'Good, good. Glad to hear it.'

He looked around before recommencing in a lower tone. 'I must admit, I agree with my wife about our visitor, Mrs Wynne-Talbot. But it's not a subject to air in public. You never know who might be listening and heaven forbid such talk got back to the Petries. It would be bound to cause offence. I hear Lady Caroline's a great fan of her nephew.'

'The lady certainly does seem very reserved but as you say she'll probably grow into her role.'

'She's a looker there's no doubt. One sees why Wynne-Talbot was attracted to her. Petrie's asked me to organise a hunting party up at Horton Plains. We've a few others coming along. A chap from Romania called Count Ranescu, and his wife among them.'

De Silva attempted not to look blank. He had no idea where Romania was and made a mental note to ask Jane. She was bound to know and she would probably know the names of its capital city, its mountains and its major rivers too. Geography was a subject she had particularly enjoyed teaching her pupils in her days as a governess.

Clutterbuck lowered his voice. 'Romania fought on our

side in the Great War and it's still one of our allies, but the Foreign Office chaps are worried that Germany's taking too much of an interest in the place. It has substantial oil reserves and an expanding arms industry. The Powers that Be want to keep an eye on developments and when they heard that Ranescu was coming to Ceylon for a spot of hunting, Petrie was told to play host and cultivate him. Apparently he's got his finger in a lot of pies.'

He tapped the ash from his cigarette onto the ground. 'Our other guest's a fellow called Aubrey. He approached me not long ago asking if there was a party he could tag along with. He's on leave from his regiment in Calcutta. Came here to see a bit of Ceylon before he goes back to England. Petrie had no objection so I told him he could join us. He seems to have done a lot of hunting in India so he should be a decent shot.'

He paused and looked at de Silva shrewdly. 'Not a hunting man, are you?'

'Not really.'

De Silva refrained from adding how distasteful he found the habit of slaughtering game in the name of sport. It was an unpleasant fact of life and the British administration was unlikely to abandon its lucrative system of selling hunting licences in the foreseeable future.

'To tell you the truth,' replied Clutterbuck, 'I'm not as fond of it as I used to be. These days I'd be satisfied with shooting for the pot – duck, snipe, that kind of thing. But I expect our visitors will be after bigger trophies.'

He dropped his cigarette end on the grass and ground it out under his heel. 'Right, time to return to the ladies.'

De Silva excused himself to pay a call of nature and was on his way back when he noticed Ralph and Helen Wynne-Talbot walking in his direction. They were alone, deep in conversation, and some instinct made him slip into the shadow of a nearby tree to avoid meeting them. His curiosity was piqued.

The Wynne-Talbots stopped when they were close to where he stood. Although he was unable to make out what they were saying, he had the impression that their exchange wasn't amicable. Ralph Wynne-Talbot's head was very close to his wife's and he seemed impatient, speaking rapidly, emphasising his words with jabs of his finger. Helen Wynne-Talbot's delphinium-blue eyes were red-rimmed and her lovely face pale as if she had been crying. Suddenly, her husband grabbed her by the wrist. She turned her face from him and tried to pull away but he held on for a few more moments before he let her go. De Silva felt sorry for her.

He waited until they had passed on, then returned to the others, mulling over what he'd seen. He wondered what had been the cause of the problem. Whatever it was, it seemed that, in spite of their glamour, the Wynne-Talbots were not a happy couple. He considered whether he ought to mention what he'd seen to Archie Clutterbuck then decided against it. The state of the Wynne-Talbots' marriage was no one else's business.

CHAPTER 3

Torches blazed on either side of the drive leading to the Residence, illuminating its white-pillared portico. Guests were already mounting the wide steps to the grand entrance doors to be greeted by servants in white and gold livery set off by scarlet turbans.

'Goodness,' Jane whispered, gathering up the skirt of her dress as she put her foot on the lowest step. 'Florence has surpassed herself. By the look of things, this is going to be a splendid evening.'

De Silva resisted the urge to tug at his bow tie. With such a crowd, it was bound to be hot inside and, since he'd come to Nuala, he'd grown used to living in a cooler temperature than he had been accustomed to in Colombo. He fiddled with his cufflinks instead. Formal English clothing was very unsuitable in the heat; he envied Jane her cool silk.

The scent of jasmine and roses met them in the entrance hall. A receiving line that consisted of the Clutterbucks, the Petries and the Wynne-Talbots had to be negotiated before they reached the drawing room where servants awaited them with flutes of champagne on silver trays. They each accepted a glass and moved further into the room.

De Silva had never seen the Residence's drawing room before and he drew a sharp breath in admiration. It rose to the height of two storeys and was painted a pale shade of blue, the colour set off by the gleaming white marble of the pilasters that punctuated the walls at regular intervals. The intricate details of the decorative plasterwork frieze that ran round the room a few feet below the ceiling were highlighted with gilding. More gilding graced the enormous mirror that surmounted a large and magnificent fireplace with a marble surround. The furniture was antique and the rugs on the parquet floor looked to be made of the finest Kashmiri silk. He suspected that Archie Clutterbuck's faithful Labrador, Darcy, would be banned from entering such an elegant room. It didn't really look like his owner's natural habitat either. The assistant government agent was more of an outdoors man.

A couple they were acquainted with came over to greet them; they'd been talking for a few moments when de Silva heard a vaguely familiar voice behind him.

'Good evening, Inspector!'

He turned to see the local doctor, David Hebden.

'Good evening to you too, sir.'

Hebden gestured to the room. 'A marvellous place for a gathering like this, eh? I've not seen it before.'

'Nor have I. Yes, it is magnificent.'

He smiled; he was glad of the opportunity to chat to the doctor on a social occasion. Hebden had been in Nuala for even less time than he had and their paths didn't often cross. He hadn't felt they'd got off to a very good start with the Renshaw business the previous year. In case they had to work together again, it would be good to defuse any resentment on Hebden's part.

'I expect our hostess is pleased we have fine weather this evening,' Hebden went on. 'No muddy shoes on her immaculate rugs.'

De Silva nodded. Where would the British be without the weather to talk about?

'The weather was excellent for the races too, I hear. Unfortunately I was called away to see a patient up at one of the plantations and was unable to attend. Are you keeping busy, Inspector?'

'Not too busy, I'm glad to say.'

'The good people of Nuala are behaving themselves then. Excellent. Let's hope it stays that way.'

The receiving line had dispersed and the Clutterbucks and their companions were mingling with the guests. Hebden surveyed the room. 'I see a few of my patients are here. No doubt they'll all ignore my strictures on over-indulging in food and alcohol this evening. I understand the Residence kitchen lays on a good spread and Archie Clutterbuck has an excellent cellar.'

'I don't expect one night's indulgence will prove fatal.'

Hebden chuckled. 'Hopefully, you're right. I don't want to lose them too fast. I have to make a living.'

'Quite.'

Lowering his voice, Hebden glanced at the Wynne-Talbots. 'So what do you make of our honoured guests?'

'I've only met them briefly. She's much quieter than her husband but both seem very charming.'

A hesitant expression came over Hebden's face, as if he was about to betray a confidence, then it disappeared as swiftly as it had come. 'The few Australians I've met haven't been backward in coming forward. Wynne-Talbot's English, of course, but apparently he's lived there for many years and he seems to share that characteristic. He has a great future ahead of him where I'm sure it will stand him in good stead.'

He glanced once again at the group gathered around the Wynne-Talbots. 'He certainly has a marked effect on the ladies. I suppose you'd call him a handsome chap.'

'How does it go? *The glass of fashion… the observed of all observers?*'

'Hamlet? I wouldn't have put you down for an aficionado of William Shakespeare, de Silva.'

'Ah yes, my wife has me reading all kinds of authors, and she sometimes drags me along to our hostess's soirées. We were treated to readings from the plays of Shakespeare last month.'

'One of the many advantages of marriage, I'm sure — having someone to broaden one's horizons.' Hebden smiled ruefully. 'I fear I'm still looking for the right girl.'

'I'm sure we can find her for you in Nuala, Doctor Hebden.' Smiling, Jane had joined them.

Hebden raised her gloved hand to his lips. 'Good evening, Mrs de Silva. May I say how lovely you look?'

'Thank you, you may.'

The sound of a gong being struck hushed the room and dinner was announced. De Silva had never sat at a table that could accommodate quite so many people before. It stretched the length of another lofty and elegant room with floor-to-ceiling windows curtained in green velvet. The walls were painted in a pastel shade of the same colour. Four large chandeliers were spaced over the table, bathing the sparkling silverware and English porcelain in warm light; many-branched silver candelabras and bowls of yellow roses embellished the picture. Jane, who was seated half a dozen places away on the opposite side, flanked by the vicar and an elderly gentleman de Silva didn't recognise, flashed him a conspiratorial smile.

He found himself seated to the left of an elderly lady dressed in a floral pink dress that looked as if it might have come from the last century. Remembering Jane had once told him that, at a formal dinner, a gentleman always makes conversation with the lady on his right to begin with, de Silva introduced himself.

'It's a pleasure to meet you, Inspector,' the lady said with a friendly smile. 'I'm already well acquainted with your wife.'

Over a pleasantly fragrant and spicy mulligatawny soup, followed by fillet of sole dusted with parsley, he learnt that her name was Joan Buscott and she was married to the elderly gentleman sitting next to Jane. He was a senior official in the Department of Roads and Railways and shortly due to retire. They were looking forward to a peaceful existence in a bungalow in a small town by the sea called Broadstairs.

'It's in Kent,' the elderly lady informed him. 'But as your wife is English, Inspector de Silva, perhaps you know the country well?'

'I have never been, ma'am, but Jane has told me many tales about it. Let me see… Kent… the White Cliffs of Dover?'

'Well done.'

'Thank you, ma'am.'

She hesitated. 'Do you and your wife find… Oh, forgive me, I don't mean to pry.'

'No apology is needed. Yes, we have encountered disapproval in some places, but those who follow their hearts must not fear that.'

'I quite agree.'

They chatted about Nuala and then turned to discussing books until servants filed into the room to remove the empty plates from the fish course. The elderly lady smiled. 'I have so enjoyed our conversation, Inspector. I hope we meet again before Broadstairs claims my husband and me.'

'Likewise, ma'am.'

'And now, as I'm sure you know, we must change conversational partners for the rest of the meal.'

De Silva thought that Bertie Wooster might have described the lady to his left as heavy weather. He battled on gamely through the roast lamb and mango ice cream but it was a relief when Florence rose from the table to announce that it was time for the ladies to withdraw and leave the gentlemen to their port.

Bottom waistcoat buttons were undone, cigars were lit and decanters circulated. De Silva was pleased to find that one of them contained a venerable malt whisky. He'd never developed a taste for port, or wine for that matter, so at dinner he'd accepted only a small glass of the latter out of politeness. Now, a rich, peaty smell tantalised his nostrils as he took the first sip.

'Excellent meal, eh?'

Dr Hebden had moved up to sit in the place vacated by the Broadstairs-bound Mrs Buscott. He seemed rather well greased, or was it oiled?

'Very fine.'

'You eat lamb?'

De Silva nodded. 'Those of us in Ceylon who are Buddhists follow the Theravada rule where the eating of meat is not strictly forbidden. The Buddha himself allowed his disciples to eat it at times.'

Hebden smiled affably. 'I have a lot to learn. It's far too infrequent that I spend time outside the British community, except with some of my patients and they only want to complain about their ailments.'

'Tell me, what brought you to Ceylon, sir?'

'I wanted a change of scene, I suppose. A bit of adventure and a chance to see the world. I've never been a man for cities, and when I finished medical school, the idea of mouldering away for the rest of my days in Little Snoring in the Marsh didn't appeal either. I spent a few years in Kenya then moved on here.'

De Silva frowned. Did such a place as this Little Snoring exist? Rather than show his ignorance, he'd ask Jane later. In any case, Hebden's attention was now diverted to the head of the table where Ralph Wynne-Talbot appeared to be telling his neighbours a highly amusing story.

After a moment or two, Hebden turned back. 'To look at Wynne-Talbot, you wouldn't think he had a care in the world, would you?'

'What do you mean?'

Hebden reached for a nearby decanter. De Silva suspected that by now alcohol had loosened his tongue.

'He asked to see me on the day before the races. He was worried she was in poor shape. Said she's suffered with her nerves for a long time and it's getting worse.'

'She? You mean his wife? Did she come with him?'

'No. She doesn't know he talked to me. He wanted it that way in case it alarmed her. According to him, she's terrified of treatment. Hardly surprising. It can be pretty harsh, as you may know. Wynne-Talbot's tried to reassure her no one would force her into anything she didn't want to do, but he said it's impossible to convince her.'

'So have you been able to form an opinion of your own about her condition?'

'From what I've seen, she's not a happy lady, that's for sure. This change in her life may help, or it might just make matters worse. I suggested he take her somewhere by the sea for a rest before they leave Ceylon. Give her a chance to build up her strength. He asked about pills but I told him I'd rather they steered clear of that kind of thing. Our American cousins are very keen on them – particularly barbiturates to cure insomnia and treat depressive illnesses – but we're more cautious in England. Some might say we're just less advanced but personally, I think it's a case where that's beneficial. Medical science doesn't know a great deal about the side effects of those kind of drugs yet. Quite apart from that, they would be pretty hard to obtain up here in Nuala.'

He glanced towards the head of the table again. 'Ah, Clutterbuck's getting up. I believe we're joining the ladies. You'll keep this under your hat, won't you, de Silva? I've said far more than I should.'

'Of course.'

As etiquette demanded, they waited for William Petrie and Clutterbuck to leave the room first. Both men passed with a polite nod and a brief word, but Ralph Wynne-Talbot stopped to greet them. 'Thank you for your help the other day,' he said quietly to Hebden. 'Much appreciated. I'm taking your advice and Helen seems more cheerful with the prospect of the two of us taking a quiet holiday.'

'Excellent, glad to hear it.'

Wynne-Talbot turned to de Silva. 'Inspector! It's a great pleasure to meet you again. I'm sorry we haven't had a chance to talk. I hope we can remedy that later on. I'd be most interested to hear more about your work.' He smiled. 'I'm sure you have a lot of stories to tell.'

De Silva laughed. 'Indeed I do, sir.'

Wynne-Talbot clapped him on the back. 'But I mustn't keep you gentlemen from the ladies. Shall we go?'

In the drawing room, he found Jane and they spent a while chatting with other guests. There was no dancing that evening so the party broke up shortly after eleven o'clock. He fetched Jane's wrap for her and they went outside to the Morris.

'A pleasant evening,' he remarked as they drove home under a starlit sky. 'I even managed to have a very civil conversation with Hebden.'

'Why ever shouldn't you? I'm sure he never really took offence over the Renshaw case.'

'Perhaps not. How did you get on with your neighbours?'

'Very well. Reverend Peters and I discussed the fête over the fish course. He was asking if I thought you could be persuaded to help with setting up some of the games and maybe stay on during the afternoon for anything else that needs doing.'

'I expect I can manage that.'

'Thank you, dear, that's very kind. On my other side I had Joan Buscott's husband – I saw she was sitting next to you. He's such a nice man. Not that I would expect him to be anything else when he's married to Joan. It turns out that he's fond of detective stories too, so we had plenty to chat about. He was telling me about their early years in

Ceylon as well. I'd no idea they'd lived in so many parts of the country. They came out forty years ago and his first job was to do with the construction of the railway from Kandy up to Jaffna.'

'That must have been most interesting work.'

'So he said, although he never got used to the heat up there. He was very excited to hear that Ralph Wynne-Talbot had been involved in the building of the Sydney Harbour Bridge. I think he was hoping for an opportunity to talk to him about it.'

'He may have done so. I noticed that Buscott moved to Wynne-Talbot's end of the table when you ladies retired for coffee.'

Jane frowned. 'There was one wrong note before you joined us. Helen Wynne-Talbot was extremely rude to poor Joan. Most unexpected, and it showed her in a new, and not very attractive, light.'

'How strange. I'm surprised anyone would find the need to be rude to Mrs Buscott.'

'So am I. Joan's the kindest of ladies, and very modest, even though she's extremely well connected and many people in her position would be quite the reverse. She made some perfectly innocuous remark and that Wynne-Talbot woman was quite snappish with her.'

De Silva thought of what Hebden had revealed but decided that, as he had promised to keep it confidential, he shouldn't mention the conversation, even to Jane. It was odd, though. You would think that, even in low spirits, Helen Wynne-Talbot would try to be polite to her host and hostess's guests when such a fine dinner had been arranged in her honour.

'And I'd thought she was shy,' Jane went on. 'Well, if she is, she has a strange way of showing it.'

'Never mind, I'm sure Mrs Buscott has the good sense to soar above such things.'

'To rise, dear, she's not an eagle.'

He chuckled. 'No, if she were a bird, I believe she would be something calm and gentle like a dove. Or possibly wise, like an owl, dispensing good advice.' He eased his foot off the pedal then accelerated out of the bend. 'The husband – Mr Wynne-Talbot I mean – went out of his way to be pleasant. He stopped purposely to speak to Hebden and me. He seems to be under the impression that police work is very interesting and I did not disillusion him.'

Jane reached out and tapped his knee. 'It is interesting, you know it is.'

'In your books, yes, but in life there is a great deal of time when it is perfectly dull. A good thing really. Nuala does not want murders and bank robberies all the time. Especially when there is only myself to solve them.'

'What about your sergeant and your constable? Don't forget them.'

He shrugged. 'I don't. Nadar may still be very inexperienced but his day will come. Prasanna is a bright young man and I have high hopes for him too, but he also needs time.'

A shadow flickered in the trees by the roadside and he braked as a spotted deer, followed swiftly by two more, shot out. They stopped for a moment, transfixed in the headlights, before bounding away into the trees on the other side.

Jane gasped. 'My goodness, that was close. How awful if we'd hit one of them.'

'Yes, and worse if it had been an elephant. I told you I came across one once on the road from Colombo to Kandy and had to reverse and wait until it wandered away.'

'You did. It must have been most alarming.'

'A little, but we have to live together, man and beast. They do not attack unless we attack them.'

'Or if they're hungry.'

'That too. I'm sure a hungry leopard would consider Florence Clutterbuck a plump and tasty morsel and much easier to catch than those spotted deer.'

'That's very naughty.'

'Only joking.'

They fell into a companionable silence for a while. 'One of her soirées came in useful though,' he said at last. 'I was able to impress Hebden with my knowledge of Shakespeare.'

'Oh really?'

'The speech of Ophelia's when she speaks of how much Hamlet has changed.'

'You remembered all of it?'

'Not all, just a few words. But I could see he was awe-struck.'

Jane giggled. 'Shanti, how much did you have to drink while I wasn't watching?'

'Mmm – one malt whisky? Maybe two.'

'Well, go slowly. You know you don't usually drink much and I want us to get home in one piece.'

'Oh, we will, have no fear. Not far to go now.'

They turned into their road and the Morris was soon scrunching up the drive. Jane waited for him to come round to her side of the car and open the door for her.

She stood on the drive and gazed up at the sky for a few moments.

'How beautiful the stars are tonight. I'm so glad we came here, Shanti. I don't miss Colombo in the slightest.'

'Neither do I. Give me the quiet life any day.'

Arm in arm they went inside, leaving the garden to the creatures of the night.

CHAPTER 4

A few days later, he arrived at the station to find Constable Nadar with his head resting on his desk, apparently fast asleep. De Silva cleared his throat noisily and the constable jumped to attention as if he had been bitten by a snake.

De Silva raised an eyebrow. 'Good morning.'

'Inspector, sir! Forgive me. I only closed my eyes for a few moments. My wife and I had no sleep last night. Our baby son is teething.'

'I'm sorry to hear that. If it's quiet today, I may be able to let you go early. Go and make us both some tea. That should wake you up.'

'Yes, sir.'

Nadar scuttled off to the back room and de Silva heard the sound of the Calor gas ring hissing into life and the clatter of spoons on china. 'Where's Sergeant Prasanna got to this morning?' he asked when Nadar returned a few minutes later with the tea.

'Gone to the bazaar, sir.'

'Oh? Has something happened there?'

'I'm not sure, sir.' Nadar's tone was evasive.

'Well, he'd better not be long unless he has a good reason. He has a report to write up about those bicycles that were stolen on Monday.' He took his cup. 'I'll drink this in my office. Tell Prasanna to knock when he gets here.'

'Yes, sir.'

It was odd, he thought as he sat at his desk sipping his tea. Prasanna had been behaving strangely for a week or more. He was often distracted and, at lunchtimes, he no longer dragged Nadar out to the backyard to practise cricket. Whatever was troubling him, it looked as if Nadar was in on it but unwilling to divulge any information. Surely it couldn't be anything sinister? Prasanna was always conscientious and it was impossible to believe he was dishonest. No, there must be another explanation.

A lightbulb went on in de Silva's head. A girl: that was probably it. There were many pretty girls shopping or helping on their family stalls at the bazaar. Well, if that was the answer, he hoped Prasanna's formidable mother would approve.

He had been working on his papers for several hours when there was a knock at the door.

'Come in!'

The door opened and Prasanna appeared. His expression lay somewhere between uncertainty and resolution.

'Ah, you're back. Anything of importance to tell me? Not the monkeys making a nuisance of themselves at the bazaar again? How many times do we have to remind the stallholders that we are policemen not animal tamers? Tell them to give some boys stout sticks and put them on watch ready to chase the monkeys away.'

He saw the sergeant's chest expand as he took a deep breath. 'Not the monkeys, sir. Something more serious than that.'

De Silva waited.

'I have been speaking with a lady there—'

De Silva couldn't resist tweaking his tail. 'This would be a young lady?'

Prasanna flushed. 'Yes, sir, but there is nothing improper.'

'Of course not. Please go on.'

'Her name is Kuveni and she is in great difficulties.'

De Silva nodded. 'Go on.'

'She and her family have been forced to leave their village and come to Nuala to find work.'

'Forced?'

Yes, sir, the headman of the village made their lives impossible to bear. He turned the other villagers against them and even accused Kuveni's father of stealing, which was not true.'

'Why did he want to harm them?'

'The headman is a bad man, but no one in the village will stand up to him. They are afraid of him and he has convinced them that if they cross him, evil spirits will attack them.' Prasanna's frown deepened to a scowl. 'He wanted to marry Kuveni but she did not like him and her father wouldn't order her to do so.'

'What else does this man do?'

'He makes many promises then breaks them. Kuveni believes that when government licences are needed for anything, he also lies about the cost and makes the villagers pay too much, keeping the rest for himself.'

De Silva picked up the pen on his desk and rotated it between the thumb and fingers of one hand. 'You say this girl has a family? Who is there apart from her father?'

'She has a brother, sir.'

'Can't the brother and father get together and persuade at least some of the villagers to stand up to this headman?'

Prasanna shook his head hopelessly. 'The father has been so troubled by the situation that he is ill and cannot work, let alone fight for his family.'

De Silva sighed. Corruption was a problem in the villages. The government agents and their assistants were responsible for rooting it out, but many of the jungle villages were very remote. What went on in them wasn't readily ascertained and unscrupulous headmen took advantage of the fact.

'If Kuveni's brother goes back to the village while the headman is in charge, she is afraid of what will happen to him. Her father needs to be looked after and she doesn't want to be left to manage all alone.'

'That's understandable. So she has asked for our help?'

'She has, sir, but I am not sure what to do for the best. If I go to the village and see the headman, he may deny everything.'

De Silva stopped turning the pen and tapped his chin with it. 'You're right up to a point. The headman will probably swear he's doing nothing wrong, but a visit might encourage him to be a little more honest. However, that will be of no help to your friend. How are she and her brother making ends meet at the moment?'

'Kuveni works for one of the sari makers in the bazaar. She has very nimble fingers and has learnt to sew and embroider to a good standard already. Her brother, his name is Vijay, used to help their father hunting and growing millet. Now he works in the bazaar delivering vegetables for some of the stallholders.'

'So, as we agree that a visit to the headman won't automatically solve your friend's problem, we must approach it another way. The assistant government agent is up at Horton Plains at the moment leading a hunting party, but when he comes back to Nuala, I will speak to him. He may be able to assist us. There will be records of the licences this headman has applied for and they may help us to uncover his bad practices. If there has been no official inspection of the village for a while, Mr Clutterbuck may see fit to arrange one. It might frighten the headman into mending his ways.'

Prasanna looked doubtful. 'Kuveni says he is a ruthless man, sir. I am not sure he will be easy to frighten.'

'We shall see.'

De Silva picked up the pen again and made a few notes

on the pad of paper in front of him. When he had finished, he replaced the cap and looked up at Prasanna with searching eyes. 'You're sure this friend of yours is telling you the truth? The assistant government agent will be angry if we raise the alarm for no reason.'

Prasanna's brow furrowed. 'I'm sure, sir.'

'Very well, leave it with me. You may tell your friend that I'll speak to Mr Clutterbuck and we'll go on from there.'

'Thank you, sir.'

'Now, put this out of your mind for the moment and go and do your work.'

After the door closed behind Prasanna, de Silva glanced at the clock on the wall. It would probably be best to telephone the Residence after lunch now, to find out when they expected Archie Clutterbuck back from Horton Plains.

He stood up, went to the window and watched the bustle of activity in the street. The inhabitants of Nuala were going about their business – working in offices; buying and selling goods; visiting their families and friends and enjoying all kinds of entertainments. Whenever his work took him to one of the villages, the contrast always gave him the feeling that a time machine had transported him back fifty years.

The contrast wasn't only in the quieter pace of life. As was general in Ceylon, people in Nuala believed in astrology. They didn't like to take important decisions until they had consulted an astrologer to ascertain which day would be the most propitious for their plans. But in the villages, belief in otherworldly powers went far beyond that. Dark superstitions and the fear of arousing the malice of the spirit world were powerful methods of control for an unscrupulous headman.

He returned to his desk and spent a few more minutes on his papers until the telephone interrupted him. He picked up the receiver; it was a call from one of Clutterbuck's staff at the Residence.

'Inspector de Silva here.'

'Thank goodness I've caught you, Inspector. I was afraid you would have left for lunch. Mr Clutterbuck needs to see you immediately.'

The urgency of the man's tone left de Silva puzzled. Clutterbuck must be back earlier than he had anticipated and this was an unusually peremptory summons. 'Then please tell him I will be with him very soon.'

'He's not at the Residence, Inspector.'

'Oh?'

'He's still at Horton Plains. He's sending some of his shikari trackers to meet you at the start of the road up there.'

De Silva was very puzzled now. 'I'll set off shortly, but may I ask what this is about?'

'There's been an accident.'

'A serious one I take it?'

'I'm afraid so. Mrs Wynne-Talbot fell from the precipice early this morning. Her body hadn't been found when Mr Clutterbuck sent the message, but we must assume she's dead.'

CHAPTER 5

The trackers waited for him at the place where the road to Horton Plains became so steep that de Silva was heartily relieved to be able to spare the Morris's protesting engine any further torment. Mounted on stocky ponies, they had brought a spare one for de Silva. He hauled himself into the saddle and they set off up the narrow road.

It wasn't long before he wished he had a better head for heights. As the road snaked up through low, scrubby forest in a series of alarmingly tight hairpin bends, he averted his eyes from the sheer drop a few yards from the line of ambling ponies. Once, a monkey leapt from a nearby bush and, gibbering furiously, scampered across their path. De Silva's pony shied and the reins slipped through his sweating palms. He quickly gathered them again and the animal settled but his heart beat faster for several minutes.

Eventually, they left the forest behind and reached the vast, grassy expanse of the Plains. Released from anxiety, de Silva once more focused his mind on his destination. World's End was the most famous spot at Horton Plains: a precipice where the ground dropped away for almost four thousand feet to the jungle below. The view, when it was not shrouded in mist, was legendary. But World's End was a dangerous place for the unwary. One false step was all that was needed for a person to plunge to their death and it was known that several had, including, apparently, the hapless Mrs Wynne-Talbot.

He frowned. Surely Clutterbuck and William Petrie would have warned their guests to be on their guard? The view was magnificent but it could be enjoyed from a few paces back if there was any danger of losing one's balance. On his own visits, he had always stopped a few feet short of the drop.

His questioning of his guides had produced very little extra information. All they had to tell him was that the accident had occurred around dawn. Helen Wynne-Talbot had been seen standing at the edge of the plateau, then she had fallen. His mind went back to the argument between the Wynne-Talbots at the racecourse. Had Helen Wynne-Talbot fallen accidentally or had she jumped, distraught after a fresh quarrel? It was a tragic explanation that he couldn't dismiss out of hand, but he would have to tread carefully. The poor lady's husband was bound to be very distressed. He must be careful not to step on the Petries' toes, too. According to Florence Clutterbuck, Lady Caroline was very fond of her nephew, even though it wasn't clear that they had known each other long.

William Petrie was more of an unknown quantity. Socially, he seemed easy-going and kindly but there was usually more than one side to a man. Petrie wouldn't have risen as high as he had in the colonial service on affability alone. Probably he would dislike showing any weakness. He might also be angry at such an unpleasant interruption to the hunting party. Particularly as he wanted this Count Ranescu in a receptive mood.

Enjoying the gentler terrain of the flat, grassy ground, the ponies trotted along confidently. A herd of sambhur, watched over by a stag with magnificent antlers, stopped grazing and galloped away as they approached. Half a mile on, they left the ponies with one of the shikaris and continued on foot.

At a height of more than seven thousand feet above sea

level, the air was thinner than de Silva was used to and he found keeping up with the shikaris strenuous. Soon, he felt as if a giant hand had fixed an iron band around his forehead and was slowly tightening it.

The path left the grasslands and plunged into another forest, this time a denser one. Clouds of vapour wreathed the gnarled, moss-encrusted trees, contriving to leach the colour from the orchids and other epiphytes that had taken up precarious residence on their bark. The high altitude made the air chilly and damp. It moulded itself to de Silva's body like a ghostly overcoat and he felt cold and miserable.

Further on, high banks, veined with bulbous tree roots, rose on either side making it essential to walk in single file. A powerful smell of earth and decay filled de Silva's nostrils. They started to walk over large boulders, the rock polished smooth by the waters of a now dry river. An incautious step trapped his foot and he grimaced with pain as he wrenched it out and limped on.

He gave a sigh of relief when the boulder-strewn path ended and they reached the first viewpoint at the place called Little World's End. There, they paused briefly to catch their breath before going on; ten minutes later, the hunting party's camp came into sight, pitched about sixty yards from the precipice at World's End.

Archie Clutterbuck saw him first and hurried over.

'De Silva! You made good time; well done. Terrible business. William Petrie's not a happy man. Not at all the way that he wanted the expedition to turn out. Poor Mrs Wynne-Talbot just went over the side. Didn't stand a chance.'

'Did you see it happen?'

Clutterbuck shook his head. 'Fast asleep in my tent. These long days out in the fresh air always poleaxe me. No, it was Major Aubrey who saw her go. Says he didn't sleep well – got up for a smoke outside his tent around dawn.

He noticed Helen Wynne-Talbot was up and on her own. Thought she must have slept badly too. She was standing at the edge of the precipice and he assumed she was admiring the view – as you probably know, it's particularly fine at sunrise. He could hardly believe his eyes when she just stepped out into thin air.'

De Silva's brow furrowed. 'Suicide?'

'Hard to credit it was anything else, unless she was sleepwalking, and don't the medics say that even then a person has an instinct for self-preservation?'

'I believe they do. How is Mr Wynne-Talbot taking the news?'

'Much as you would expect – stiff upper lip and all that – but there's bound to be a lot bubbling under the surface. He had no idea anything had happened until Aubrey raised the alarm. Lady Caroline's very distressed and naturally worried about her nephew. You'll need to handle both of them carefully.'

The trace of an apologetic smile crossed his face. 'Forgive me, de Silva. I appreciate you don't need me to tell you how to do your job.' He jabbed a hand through his thick, white hair. 'This ghastly business has us all rattled.'

William Petrie emerged from one of the tents and walked over to join them.

'Good morning, Inspector. My apologies for dragging you up here at such short notice.'

'Please think nothing of it, sir. I'm very sorry to hear what's happened. May I offer my condolences?'

'Thank you.'

Petrie's calm demeanour gave nothing away. 'Has Clutterbuck filled you in?'

'I understand Major Aubrey saw Mrs Wynne-Talbot fall.'

'That's correct. The rest of the party was still asleep, including myself and my wife. She's extremely upset by all this so she's resting at the moment. I'd prefer it if she wasn't disturbed.'

'Of course, but if I may, I'd like to see the place where the lady fell and then ask the other members of the party a few questions.'

'By all means, but apart from Aubrey, I doubt they'll be able to tell you anything of importance.'

De Silva nodded politely. 'All the same, I would like to speak to them.'

The three men walked away from the tents and had soon covered the short distance to the precipice. Beyond the edge, milky fog swirled, completely obscuring the jungle far below. It was a feature of World's End that the view was only visible for a few hours in the morning before the heat from the jungle rose to meet the humid air of the plateau.

'Aubrey tells me she stood there before she fell.' Clutterbuck indicated a spot where a tuft of parched grass grew between a few loose stones.

De Silva studied the spot. It was possible that Helen Wynne-Talbot had stumbled, but unlikely. The stones were small and it shouldn't have been difficult for her to right herself. At sunrise, the visibility would have been good. Could she have been disorientated on waking, or fuddled with drink? If the violent argument he had witnessed at the races was a regular feature of the Wynne-Talbots' relationship, she might have been in the habit of turning to the bottle for comfort. A temporary relief that would probably only make their marital difficulties worse in the long run.

'Have you seen enough, Inspector?' An impatient edge sharpened William Petrie's voice.

'For the present, sir. I'd like to speak to Major Aubrey now.'

Aubrey sat on a camp stool in his tent. De Silva smelt whisky on the stuffy air. A glass and a half-empty bottle stood on a low table. The major followed de Silva's glance.

'Needed a stiffener,' he said dismissively. 'It's not every day a chap wakes up to something like this. Of course, you can't be in the army without seeing death close up, but there one's prepared for it.'

De Silva nodded. 'It must have been a shock.'

'It was.'

Clutterbuck cleared his throat. 'Well, gentlemen, shall we sit outside? Not much room in here.'

Aubrey uncurled himself from his stool and stood up. He was in his mid-thirties, athletic in appearance and just over six feet tall, overtopping de Silva by several inches. His dark hair and chiselled good looks reminded de Silva of the American actor, Clark Gable, one of whose films he had seen recently with Jane at the cinema. Instead of Gable's smooth confidence, however, Aubrey radiated tension and strain. Hardly surprising in the circumstances, reflected de Silva. He remembered that Aubrey was on leave from his post in Calcutta. Presumably it was exposure to the Indian sun that had tanned and weathered his skin.

Clutterbuck led them to a table in the shade of a clump of trees. 'I suggest we have something to eat.' He snapped his fingers to summon a servant. 'Coffee and eggs and be sharp about it.'

De Silva frowned. Clutterbuck must be rattled, he didn't usually play the colonial master so blatantly. With a sigh, he inwardly predicted that the servant would serve camp coffee. Revolting stuff that tasted of chicory and had probably never encountered a coffee bean. He suspected that Major Aubrey would have preferred more whisky and he wouldn't have minded one himself. The damp chill of the journey still permeated his bones.

They sat down and he brought out his notebook and pen from his knapsack and laid them on the table in front of him.

'There's not much I can tell you, Inspector,' Aubrey

began. 'I don't sleep soundly as a rule – army training I suppose – and it's not unusual for me to wake at dawn.'

'I understand you decided to get up for a smoke?'

'That's right. I pulled on my trousers and a shirt and went outside. The moon had set and the sky was turning grey. There was a faint line of red on the eastern horizon.'

He stopped as a servant laid out cups on the table and poured coffee. The smell of chicory rose to de Silva's nostrils. Two more servants arrived with plates and cutlery followed by fried eggs. At least those were cooked as de Silva liked them, soft yolks and a little burnt around the edges.

Aubrey waited until the servants had gone before he continued. 'At first I didn't realise anyone else was up. I put a plug of tobacco in my pipe, lit it and wandered towards the precipice to take a look at the view. I'd heard it's at its best at dawn.'

He paused and drank some of his coffee. 'That was when I noticed Mrs Wynne-Talbot. She had her back to me and she was standing right at the edge of the precipice. I wasn't sure what to do. I assumed she'd come out to admire the sunrise as I had and I didn't want to alarm her in case she stumbled. She must have heard me because she turned round. I wished her good morning and said something about the light but I don't think she had a clue what I was talking about. She had the strangest expression on her face, as if she was listening to a sound from far away.'

He stopped and they all waited a few moments.

'And then?' enquired de Silva at last.

'Then she simply turned to face the drop, and was gone.'

'And how long do you estimate the whole episode lasted?'

'A minute, possibly two, but that's a guess.' A note of sarcasm came into his voice. 'I'm not in the habit of witnessing suicides so I forgot to look at my watch.'

De Silva ignored the jibe and jotted down a quick note.

'Were you acquainted with Mrs Wynne-Talbot before the expedition?'

Aubrey shook his head. 'Never met her or her husband until we started out from Nuala.'

'Clutterbuck, Lady Caroline and I are the only people on the expedition who'd met the Wynne-Talbots before,' William Petrie intervened.

'I don't believe I exchanged more than two words with her once we had met,' Aubrey added.

'Did she seem to be enjoying herself?'

'Hard to say,' said Petrie. 'My wife's nephew always takes the lead. Helen is,' he paused, '*was*, a very reserved lady.'

'I appreciate none of you knew her well, but was there anything unusual about her behaviour yesterday?' De Silva lowered his voice. 'Did anything seem amiss between her and her husband? Was she drinking more than usual?'

Petrie's eyebrows went up and de Silva was afraid he had been presumptuous. 'There was nothing unusual about her behaviour and no argument with Wynne-Talbot,' the government agent said firmly. 'As for drink, from what I've seen of her, she hardly touched the stuff. A small sherry before dinner at most.'

De Silva jotted down a few more notes. It was always possible that Mrs Wynne-Talbot drank more in private than she did in public, but suggesting that might further arouse Petrie's displeasure and get them no further forward. He put down his pen.

'Thank you, Major Aubrey. I don't think I need detain you any longer.'

Aubrey pushed back his stool and stood up. 'I'm sorry I can't be of more help.' He turned to William Petrie. 'I suppose you'll be calling a halt to the expedition now, sir?'

Petrie nodded. 'In the circumstances, it would be inappropriate to continue.'

'I understand.'

'When Inspector de Silva has completed his inquiries, I'll make the arrangements for departure and you'll be informed.'

'Thank you, sir.'

'Decent enough fellow,' Petrie remarked quietly as Aubrey returned to his tent. 'Even if he does seem a little too fond of the bottle. Still, today he has some excuse.'

'Do you know much about his history?'

'Very little. He mentioned to my wife that he grew up in Devon. He also told her his regiment has been stationed in India for several years, but he and I talked mainly about shooting, and not a great deal about that. I didn't want to spare him too much time. In effect, Aubrey invited himself on this expedition and it was up to him to make himself agreeable. My brief was to see to it that the Ranescus had a good time.'

He scowled. 'One shouldn't speak ill of the dead, but Helen Wynne-Talbot turned out to be a most unfortunate addition to the party. Of course, I won't say that in my wife's hearing.'

A twig cracked and he looked up. 'Ah, here comes Countess Ranescu. By the way, she's Italian, originally from Rome I believe, but her English is flawless.'

De Silva was transfixed. The first sight of the countess was enough to take any man's breath away. Whereas the tragic Mrs Wynne-Talbot's beauty had been remote and ethereal, the countess was utterly beguiling. A pair of immaculately tailored khaki trousers and a cream silk shirt set off her lissom figure to perfection. An abundance of dark, wavy hair framed a vivacious face with eyes of such a dark blue that they were almost black. At the moment, their expression was solemn, but it was easy to imagine how they would sparkle when a less sombre occasion did not forbid merriment.

Petrie and Clutterbuck scraped back their chairs in the

dust and jumped to their feet; de Silva followed suit.

'I hope I am not interrupting your talk, gentlemen.' The countess's seductively accented voice lingered over the words.

'Not at all, Countess.' William Petrie hurried to greet her and she held out her hand for him to kiss. Archie Clutterbuck straightened his tie and bowed. She rewarded him with a charming smile that revealed neat, flawlessly white teeth, then turned her attention to de Silva.

'Ah, the famous Inspector de Silva.'

To his surprise, de Silva felt a flush creep up his neck in a way that he had not experienced since his youth. He bowed. 'You do me too much credit, Countess Ranescu.'

'I'm sure I do not, Inspector. Everyone speaks very highly of you and your skill in solving mysteries and unmasking villainy. But how sad we must meet in such tragic circumstances. If there is anything I can do to help, I shall be delighted, but I fear I only know what Major Aubrey has to tell.'

'But a woman's intuition is a powerful tool,' said Petrie. 'The inspector has been asking whether we noticed anything strange about Mrs Wynne-Talbot's behaviour yesterday. Can you help us?'

The countess tilted her lovely head to one side and pondered for a moment before speaking quietly.

'We had only just met so she was unlikely to confide in me, but she did seem very sad. I wondered if she and her husband had had a disagreement, or perhaps she was not as fond of hunting as he was.'

De Silva glanced at the tents scattered around the clearing. 'Which one did Mrs Wynne-Talbot sleep in?'

Petrie pointed. 'That one, and my wife's nephew has the one next to it. The tents are fairly small – it's always a problem carrying equipment all this way – so it made sense to have one person to a tent.'

'My tent is there,' said the countess, pointing with a perfectly manicured finger. 'And the count's is on the far side. The distance to poor Signora Wynne-Talbot's tent is not far, but he and I slept soundly and heard nothing.' She made a sweeping gesture with her elegant hand. 'So much fresh air, but so damp and chilly. The count suffers from a cold since we arrived here. His medicine is brandy.'

The man who just then emerged from one of the tents she had pointed to was, de Silva assumed, the count. He was as stocky as his wife was slender, with a coarse moustache tweaked into handlebars on either side of his pink, fleshy lips. With his small, fierce eyes, he reminded de Silva of a bird of prey skulking on its perch. His very evident cold had probably ruffled his feathers even more than usual.

Petrie hurried forward. 'Please come and join us, Count Ranescu. Once again, I'm so sorry about all this, especially when you're unwell.'

Ranescu acknowledged Petrie's remarks with a churlish nod. No doubt to him the death of a being with two legs instead of four was an inexcusable inconvenience. He stared at de Silva rudely. 'Who is this?'

De Silva resolved not to give the man the satisfaction of responding with anything but courtesy. 'Good morning, Count Ranescu. I am Inspector de Silva of the Nuala police, at your service.'

The count grunted. 'I suppose Petrie had to call you in, but to me the answer is obvious. The lady wished to kill herself and she succeeded.'

An awkward silence descended and de Silva hoped this wouldn't be the moment that Lady Caroline or, worse still, Ralph Wynne-Talbot chose to come out of their tents.

'I'm sure you are hungry, dearest,' the countess said quickly. 'Perhaps something can be arranged?' She smiled at William Petrie.

'Of course, of course. I should have thought of it sooner.'

Orders were barked and servants scuttled to bring up another table and more chairs. Soon the count was tucking into a large plate of eggs, which improved his mood a little but de Silva still learnt nothing from him or the countess that might throw new light on Mrs Wynne-Talbot's death.

When the count had eaten his fill, he and the countess retired to their tents.

'Count or no count,' Archie Clutterbuck muttered under his breath, 'what a beautiful woman like the countess sees in that appalling fellow I find it impossible to imagine.'

Petrie chuckled dryly. 'Oh, I'm told he has redeeming features. Several million of them. I expect they go quite some way to providing compensation for the count's lack of charm.' He shrugged. 'Otherwise, I agree with your assessment. To be perfectly honest, even if it weren't for today's unfortunate events, I'm not convinced we'd have built up any trust or respect with the count. I suppose I'll have to put up with some flak from the Powers that Be in Colombo, but I can't say I'll be sorry to see the last of him. Two consecutive days in his company are more than any sane man should be obliged to endure; one doesn't so much converse with him as get mown down by a juggernaut of tedious self-congratulation. As for his prowess with a shotgun, even though he's very fond of claiming he was brought up with a Purdey in his hands on the family estates in Romania, he couldn't hit a barn door at five paces.'

He turned to de Silva. 'Well, Inspector, you've seen the best and the worst I have to offer you. I take it you'd like to speak to my wife's nephew before wrapping things up?'

De Silva nodded.

'I'm sure I don't have to tell you to be tactful. Damned awful thing to happen to a chap. He seems to be coping but it's hard to work out if that's just skin deep, and to know how to help. Lady Caroline has taken a great liking to him and she's doing her best, but Wynne-Talbot's been acquainted with us for such a short time. To a certain extent, we probably still seem like strangers.'

'You think he may feel that?'

'I wouldn't be surprised.' He shrugged. 'My wife won't hear a word against him, and she's also delighted to have the succession restored to the direct line of the family, but as far as I'm concerned, it cuts both ways.' He levelled a serious look at them. 'I rely on what I'm about to tell you not going any further, gentlemen. Are we agreed?'

Clutterbuck and de Silva nodded. Clutterbuck spoke for both of them. 'Of course, sir.'

'Then I'll tell you that the future Lord Axford came as a bit of a surprise and, charming as he is, I still haven't quite fathomed him.'

From what de Silva knew of Petrie, it didn't surprise him that he took a more cautious view of the new addition to the family than his warm-hearted wife.

'Granted he's had a pretty unconventional life for a member of a blue-blooded family,' Petrie went on. 'My wife's eldest brother, Lionel, should have inherited the earldom, but he fell out with my father-in-law, the present earl. Lionel went to Australia twenty-five years ago and my father-in-law disinherited him. He left everything to his other son, Marcus, but then Marcus was killed in the Great War. He had no children.'

A fly landed on a few grains of sugar that had been spilt on the table and started to feed. Petrie brushed it off before continuing.

'The Axford title must pass down the male line so the heir was then a distant cousin of my wife's. My father-in-law disapproved of the title and the property being separated so he left all of the Axford estates to the cousin too.'

William Petrie cleared his throat before resuming. 'But losing both his sons hit my father-in-law hard. As he grew older, he bitterly regretted the rift with Lionel and wanted them to be reconciled, thus restoring him as the next heir to the title and estates. Sadly, by the time he came to that decision, it proved impossible to find Lionel.'

De Silva frowned as he assimilated this information.

'However, my father-in-law didn't entirely give up hope,' Petrie continued. 'He altered the provisions of his will to provide that if Lionel, or any of his male issue, were found by the time the will took effect, in other words by the time of my father-in-law's death, they would inherit in place of the cousin. Regrettably, as time went by, that eventuality seemed more and more unlikely.'

De Silva usually discounted most of the beliefs many of his countrymen held about arousing the anger of the gods, but he couldn't help thinking that the Wynne-Talbot family had been very unlucky in their family affairs. Perhaps the services of a good astrologer would have helped them avoid some of their bad decisions and the consequences that flowed from them. 'So, am I right in thinking that Mr Ralph Wynne-Talbot is Lionel's son?' he asked.

'Yes. In the early years after Lionel left England, my wife had occasional contact with him and his wife, but eventually the letters stopped, so we were very surprised when we heard from Ralph a few months ago. He explained that his father had been dead for several years but his mother had only recently died. She'd always been against making contact with the family. Apparently, Lionel had suffered with mental problems for a long time and she blamed his father's rejection of him for that.'

Another fly landed on the table and he batted it away with distaste. He looked round for a servant. 'Clean this up,' he barked irritably. His forehead puckered. 'Where was I?'

'You were speaking of Mr Wynne-Talbot's late mother, sir.'

'Ah yes. The upshot of it is that, as she was dying, she relented and told him that if he wanted to find his family, he had her blessing. She'd kept some of the letters Lady Caroline wrote to Lionel and she gave them to Ralph. Starting from there, he found out that we were living in Ceylon. As my wife is the member of the family who was always closest to Lionel, Ralph asked if he could visit us here before going on to England to be with his grandfather.'

Petrie shook his head. 'Poor fellow, I don't imagine it occurred to him that he would be doing so without his wife by his side.' He swivelled in his chair and stretched his long legs. 'I'd better go and speak to my wife. I promised her I wouldn't let you ask Ralph any questions without her being present.'

Clutterbuck and de Silva exchanged looks as Petrie walked away to Lady Caroline's tent. 'Well, I wasn't expecting that,' Clutterbuck remarked in an undertone. 'Not something to broadcast, eh, de Silva?'

'Certainly not, sir.'

'We mustn't forget, we gave our word. I'm afraid it means I'll have to leave Mrs Clutterbuck in suspense. She's intrigued to know why Lady Caroline has never mentioned her nephew in the past. What Petrie said explains it. Ah,' he lowered his voice. 'Here comes Lady Caroline with her nephew now. I'm sure I needn't remind you, but be careful what you say.'

Then why do so? De Silva suppressed a twinge of annoyance.

Studying Ralph Wynne-Talbot, he was surprised that he looked as composed as he did. The famous stiff upper lip of the British might, of course, account for it.

'Good morning, Inspector de Silva.' Lady Caroline's smile was strained and she sounded tired. 'My husband tells me you have a few questions, so my nephew and I have come to answer them but I hope you won't keep us long.'

De Silva bowed. 'I shall try not to, my lady, but first please accept my sincere condolences.'

'Shall we sit down?' asked Petrie. He drew out a chair for Lady Caroline and the party waited for her to take it before seating themselves.

'Well, fire away, Inspector,' Ralph Wynne-Talbot said flatly. He sank so low in his chair that his chin was almost resting on his chest. The fingers of his right hand beat an erratic tattoo on the armrest. Lady Caroline put her hand on his. 'If it's too painful, you don't need to talk to the inspector now, Ralph. I'm sure he will understand if you'd rather wait.'

He gave her a wan smile. 'Dear Aunt Caroline, you mustn't worry about me so. The inspector has a job to do and I oughtn't to stand in his way. As I said, Inspector, fire away.'

'If you have no objection, I'd like to start by asking you to tell me what you remember happening this morning.'

'Very well, I don't suppose there's much to say that hasn't already been said. I heard Aubrey raise the alarm around dawn and it took me a few seconds to wake up. At first, I thought he might have been attacked by a wild animal of some kind and the shikaris would go to his rescue, then I heard my wife's name and my blood turned cold.'

'You thought it might have been she who had been attacked?'

'Yes. I scrambled out of my sleeping bag as fast as I could. I'd gone to sleep in my shirt and trousers and I didn't stop to find my shoes. I ran out barefoot and there was Aubrey. He looked horrified when he saw me and started gibbering something about Helen but I couldn't make sense of it. I looked around, terrified I'd see her body.'

He stopped and moistened his lips with his tongue. Lady Caroline leant forward. 'Do you need something to drink, my dear?'

He shook his head. 'When I couldn't see her anywhere, I was afraid whatever it was had dragged her off. I shouted at Aubrey to calm down and tell me what had happened.'

His voice became husky. 'That's when he told me she'd fallen. I didn't believe him at first. I even made a joke of it, God help me. I suppose I was afraid. I said he needed to lay off the whisky or he'd be telling me he'd seen pink elephants next.' He raised his head; his eyes glistened. 'Then I realised he was telling the truth.'

'You say you were afraid,' de Silva said gently. 'Was that because you were already worried about your wife?'

Reluctantly, Ralph Wynne-Talbot nodded. 'Yes, although I never thought she'd do anything like this. She'd been unhappy for a while. We'd been expecting a child and she lost it. I tried to help her get over that but it was very hard for her. I took her to doctors; they said she needed time. When she agreed to leave Australia, I hoped a new life in England would help.' He raised his hands in a gesture of hopelessness. 'I'll always believe I should have done more. I just didn't know what.'

Lady Caroline stood up and patted his arm. 'Well done, my dear.'

She turned to de Silva. 'Have you heard enough now, Inspector? I think my nephew needs to rest.'

'Of course. And once again, sir, I'm sorry to trouble you at such a sad time.'

Petrie stood up 'I'll join you in a moment or two, my dear,' he said.

He waited until his wife and her nephew had walked away before turning to de Silva. 'Thank you, Inspector. I expect you'll want to be getting on with the job of finding the body now. Clutterbuck? A word if you please before I go.'

The two men walked a little way off and spoke briefly. Unable to hear the gist of the conversation, de Silva waited for Clutterbuck to return. It had been an uncomfortable hour and he was glad it was over.

The body would need to be found and examined, of course, but it was hard to believe that Helen Wynne-Talbot's death was anything but suicide. It was a pity that no one except Major Aubrey had seen her jump, but why would he lie? All the same, it had always been his professional opinion that one should leave no stone unturned. His time in the force in Colombo, indeed all his experience in the police service, had convinced him that nothing should ever be taken on trust. It was extraordinary how often what seemed at first to be an open-and-shut case proved to be nothing of the sort when you dug deeper. He would like to try and find out a bit more about Aubrey to satisfy himself the man was reliable. Maybe learn more about the Ranescus too, even though it seemed unlikely that anything he discovered would change his view of what had happened at dawn that morning.

Clutterbuck returned and sat down heavily. 'Well done, de Silva. Dashed delicate situation. Fortunately, Petrie didn't have any complaints about how you handled it. Grisly business finding the body, I'm afraid, but see to it as soon as you can, will you?'

'I'll get onto it straight away, sir.'

'Best get the funeral over as quickly as possible and return to normal. Although I don't suppose life will be normal for poor Wynne-Talbot for a long time.'

'Quite.'

Clutterbuck sighed. 'Well, I think that about wraps everything up. I'll tell a couple of the shikaris to guide you back.'

He frowned. 'One thing did strike me as a bit odd. One of them has gone missing. Disappeared in the night it seems, and none of the others admit to knowing anything about him. Perhaps there was some kind of argument, but I didn't hear anything and their camp isn't all that far away from our tents. It's most unusual for a shikari not to stay around to get paid.'

CHAPTER 6

Now that de Silva knew the worst to expect, the journey down the mountainside seemed easy. The shikaris left him where he had parked the Morris and he drove back to Nuala. It was late afternoon by the time he arrived. In the bazaar, the few traders who had not already packed away their stalls drowsed in the shade or smoked the clay pipes filled with dark, pungent tobacco that many of the men favoured. Half-naked children darted between the traffic of bullock carts, handcarts, and rickshaws. On a patch of dusty ground, a dozen or so boys were playing a noisy game of cricket. De Silva wondered if that was how Sergeant Prasanna had learnt to love the game as a boy.

At the station, there was no sign of him. Constable Nadar was once again slumped over his desk asleep. De Silva sighed. He didn't know how long babies went on teething for but he hoped Nadar's son wouldn't take too much longer. In his office, the same pile of post that he had been perusing that morning lay on his desk. He glanced through the letters he hadn't had time to read but there was nothing that couldn't wait.

The window must have been closed all day and the temperature in the room was hot enough to cook eggs. He went to the switch and turned on the ceiling fan but it made very little difference and the monotonous swish of its blades made him feel sleepy too. There was no point sending anyone out to look for Mrs Wynne-Talbot's body until tomorrow anyway. He may as well let Nadar go off duty and then lock up. Returning to the front office, he shook the constable awake and, after a brief admonishment, sent him home.

* * *

'What a dreadful thing to happen,' said Jane sadly as they sat on the verandah that evening and watched the sun go down. 'It's tragic when anyone dies prematurely, but poor Helen Wynne-Talbot was so young. How is her husband taking it?'

'Very shocked as you would expect. It appears he knew she was suffering from depression, but not that there was a real risk she would take her own life.'

'Has her body been found?'

'Not yet. Clutterbuck's put me in charge of organising the search for it. It won't be easy but there are a few roads and small settlements down in the valley below World's End. We'll have to enlist the help of the villagers.'

'Will you go yourself?'

He shook his head. 'It will be good experience for Prasanna and Nadar. Do them no harm to face the grimmer side of policing.' He raised an eyebrow. 'Anyway, Nadar should benefit from getting out of the office and taking some exercise. Every time I turn my back on him, he falls asleep.'

'You make him sound like the dormouse.'

'The dormouse?'

'You know, in *Alice in Wonderland.*'

'Ah yes.' He remembered it was one of the books Jane had brought with her, a treasured volume from her childhood.

'But without the teapot, of course.'

De Silva chuckled as he pictured Nadar's plump personage wedged in a teapot.

'Why's he so tired? I hope you don't make him work too hard.'

'I think that would be impossible. No, it's his baby son. He's teething and Nadar says he and his wife get no sleep.'

'Oh dear.'

Jane sighed. 'I hope there won't be a lot of gossip about Helen Wynne-Talbot, not just for her husband's sake but Lady Caroline must be very distressed too. I expect she'd rather as few people as possible know what's happened.'

'Let's hope she gets her wish but I'm afraid she may not. The Wynne-Talbots have made quite a splash in Nuala and people will wonder where she is.'

She nodded. 'Unfortunately you're probably right and, if past history is anything to go by, one won't need to look far for the chief source of gossip.'

'Florence Clutterbuck?'

'Yes. But perhaps Archie will manage to keep her quiet.'

De Silva grinned 'I doubt it. It's always the wife who wears the shorts in the household.'

Jane pulled a cushion out from under her arm and threw it at him. 'What nonsense, and it's trousers not shorts.'

De Silva placed the cushion on the floor. 'Ah well, let's talk of something more cheerful.'

'Agreed.' She thought for a moment. 'There's an American film coming to the Casino that I'd like to see.'

'What's it called?'

'*Footlight Parade*. The choreographer is Busby Berkeley so there'll be lots of wonderful dancing and it stars James Cagney and Joan Blondell.'

'I thought he played gangsters.'

Usually he does but this time he's a theatre impresario. He started out in vaudeville, so he should be able to dance.'

'That's fine. I enjoyed *42nd Street* so let's try it.'

His foot started to tap and he hummed the big number from the film – rather tunelessly if the truth was told.

Jane winced. She loved music and was glad he liked it too but he was a better audience than performer. Charitably, she had decided that the difference between East and West was probably to blame for his perilous hold on the melodies of most of the western songs he sang.

Dusk turned swiftly to darkness and, little by little, the stars came out, studding the velvet-black sky like diamonds. Jane and de Silva slipped into a companionable silence. This was one of his favourite times of day, even more precious than usual after such a melancholy one. The smell of spices wafted from the direction of the kitchen, reminding him he had eaten nothing since that camp meal of eggs and horrible coffee.

Jane picked up the week's copy of the *Nuala News* and folded it over. 'We've half an hour before dinner. Do help me finish this crossword. I've been stuck on fourteen down all afternoon.'

CHAPTER 7

Early the following week, de Silva drove to the Residence to make his report to Archie Clutterbuck. Waiting in the cool of the spacious hall, he enjoyed the scent of the vase of roses someone had put on the central table. No doubt it was one of the servants. Unlike Jane, Florence didn't believe in doing anything in the house herself, even such a pleasant job as arranging flowers.

The servant who had gone to announce him returned to show him through to the study. As soon as he had opened the door, the man departed hastily and de Silva soon saw why. What appeared to be a small black and white household mop darted at him making a noise like a troop of langur monkeys in a bad temper.

'Angel! Stop that at once, you little…'

The mop cocked its head to one side and emitted a low growl. Behind it, de Silva saw the assistant government agent. His expression was thunderous and, by his side, his elderly Labrador, Darcy, wagged his tail with an air of weary resignation.

'I didn't know you had purchased a new dog, sir.'

'I haven't. The little blighter belongs to Mrs Clutterbuck. She calls it Angel although Beelzebub would be a better appellation. Poor old Darcy's nose is completely out of joint. He's used to peace and quiet. My wife insisted we have the wretch today while she's out doing good works.'

He fondled Darcy's ears and the old dog leant against his thigh with a grunt. 'Not much longer eh, old chap? She'll be home soon.'

He straightened up. 'Now, what have you got to tell me, Inspector? Any sign of Mrs W-T's body?'

'Not yet, I'm afraid. My men have spent many hours searching and drafted in villagers to help, but there's no trace of her.'

Clutterbuck sucked air through his teeth. 'William Petrie has had to go back to Kandy but I doubt Lady Caroline or Wynne-Talbot will leave until the lady's found, so pull out the stops, won't you?' He frowned. 'I hope you told your chaps to keep this under their hats?'

'Of course, sir.'

'Unfortunately, someone didn't. I've already had to take the editor of the *Nuala News* to task. Luckily I spotted the article and had time to keep it away from Lady Caroline and Wynne-Talbot but heaven knows how many other people saw it. All most regrettable. No one likes to see their family mishaps splashed over the front page. If Lady Caroline and Wynne-Talbot do hear of it, William Petrie will have something to say about the lapse and no mistake.'

How the British liked their understatement, de Silva thought wryly. Helen Wynne-Talbot's death was more than a mishap. He wondered if it was unfair to suspect that Florence Clutterbuck was the cause of her husband's discomfiture.

'Are you convinced it was suicide, sir?'

Clutterbuck looked bemused. 'Are you suggesting it might be something else?'

'Probably not, but I would be more satisfied if someone other than Major Aubrey had seen the lady jump.'

'I suppose we don't really know much about him,' Clutterbuck conceded, stroking his chin. 'Is there anything that makes you doubtful apart from that?'

'Mrs Wynne-Talbot seemed a quiet lady, but it's a long way from that to being suicidal. We haven't had the opportunity of checking whether her husband's account of her depression is true.' He didn't mention what Hebden had told him about Ralph Wynne-Talbot's visit. It would be up to the doctor to agree to reveal that he had breached his duty of confidence. 'I'd just like to be convinced that Major Aubrey is a reliable witness. I'm also somewhat troubled by what you told me about one of the shikaris.'

A frown creased Clutterbuck's brow. 'What was that?'

'You said one of them had disappeared in the night and that it was unusual.'

'Ah yes. You think he might have seen something Aubrey didn't want us to know? Goodness, de Silva, this is all a bit too cloak and dagger, don't you think?'

'All the same, I'd like to know more about Major Aubrey.'

He saw Clutterbuck stiffen but he didn't intend to back down. Being an Englishman and an officer wasn't necessarily a guarantee of probity.

Clutterbuck relaxed. 'The belt and braces approach, eh? Well, I suppose you proved its worth in that Renshaw business last year. The fellows in Colombo may be able to telegraph the army office in Calcutta.' He gave de Silva a steely look. 'But I've little doubt they'll confirm his bona fides and that will be the end of the matter.'

'Would Colombo be able to tell us anything about the count and his wife?' de Silva asked as an afterthought.

Clutterbuck's face reddened. 'Dammit, de Silva, you're going too far. The expedition's already been a disaster from that point of view and if it gets back to Ranescu that we've been asking questions about him, relations will sour even more. Petrie and the governor would have my hide.'

Excited by Clutterbuck's raised voice, the household mop jumped up and capered about, yapping furiously.

'Silence! Dratted creature.'

The mop retreated to its basket in a corner of the room and started to pant, showing a sliver of pink tongue. It had a little slit of a mouth and pair of black button eyes, half-concealed by overhanging hair that gave it an air of permanent disapproval. Jane had often told him about the British theory that people grew to look like their dogs. Angel's appearance was thought-provoking.

'My apologies for raising it, sir.'

Clutterbuck sighed. 'I ought to apologise too, de Silva. That little brute's been getting on my nerves all morning. Look, I really can't countenance making inquiries about Count Ranescu and his wife in any official capacity, but I suppose we could go to the library here. I believe there are some volumes of the *Almanach de Gotha* somewhere on the shelves – the *Almanach de Gagas* as my father used to call it.'

Clutterbuck chortled and de Silva made a mental note to ask Jane why the remark would be amusing. 'My predecessor was very keen on researching that kind of thing and boning up on the lineage of aristocratic families – we haven't cancelled the subscription as it can be useful if a bigwig visits – but it's not my bag. Give me a fishing rod or a gun any day. A chap needs to get out in the fresh air and take a bit of exercise after a day stewing over a hot desk. *Mens sana in corpore sano* I always say.'

Another question for Jane.

'As for you, you can stay in here.' Clutterbuck shook a finger at the mop. 'Come along, Darcy. We'll take you with us.'

Clearly relieved to be free of his canine companion, Darcy led the way down a long corridor lined with faded watercolours of misty lakes and mountains.

The library was far from being as grand as the one at the Crown Hotel that de Silva had once entered. Clutterbuck went to the window and pushed the heavy damask drapes aside, letting sunshine flood into the room. The bright light showed up the dust hanging in the air and lying on surfaces. De Silva noticed that most of the spines of the leather-bound books that lined the shelves had lost their glossy patina and their gold tooling was dulled by age.

'A pity it doesn't get more use,' remarked Clutterbuck, surveying the room. 'My wife's a keen reader but she's more for Agatha Christie than the classics. D'you read much, de Silva?'

'Yes, sir. I find it helps my understanding of English.'

'Quite so.' He went to a shelf. 'Now, this is the most recent one, so it may help us.'

He hauled out a heavy tome, took it to the desk and began to leaf through the crackling pages.

'Here we are,' he said after a few moments. 'Count Victor Zoltan Ranescu, born 1872 Bucharest.' His finger moved down the page. 'Married 1897, Princess Maria Cristina von Donmar – born 1875, Spezia.'

'So that means that Countess Ranescu must be sixty years old,' said de Silva, frowning.

Clutterbuck chuckled. 'The old dog! If the lady I've spent the last few days with is sixty, I'm a monkey's uncle. I wonder where Ranescu found her. Unless he's newly widowed or divorced, one presumes that the real countess is at home looking after the family estates, blissfully ignorant, one hopes, of her husband's antics.'

He closed the book and put it back in its place on the shelves. 'Well, it's none of our business and we certainly don't want to stir up a hornets' nest by asking questions now.' Absentmindedly, he brushed some dust from his sleeve. 'Let's go back to my study. A whisky before you go?'

'Thank you, sir. That would be most welcome.'

They walked back to the study where a scene of destruction met their eyes. Two of the cushions from the conker-brown leather sofa lay on the floor, feathers spilling from their torn covers. The mop glared balefully at them over the edge of a third one that was gripped between its teeth.

'Dammit! I should have known better than to leave the little blighter unsupervised.' He wrestled the cushion from Angel who trotted off to his basket with an insouciant air. 'I'd give him to the servants to look after when Mrs Clutterbuck's out but he knows how to get on chairs and steal food. He got into the boot room the other day too. One of the servants had left my best brogues out for polishing. He swears he left the door shut but now my brogues have teeth marks and one of the tongues is chewed to pieces.'

Scooping up stray feathers, he stuffed them back into the mangled cushions and put them on the sofa. 'No good complaining.'

He sneezed noisily. 'My wife won't hear a word against him. Now, how about that whisky?'

As de Silva drove away from the Residence half an hour later, he felt a pang of guilt that he hadn't mentioned Kuveni, the girl Prasanna was concerned about. But with the Wynne-Talbot business unresolved, it probably wouldn't have been a good time.

He sighed. Always the British and their concerns came first. He hoped Prasanna wouldn't feel too let down.

CHAPTER 8

'Have you had a good day, dear?' Jane smiled at him from her rattan chair on the verandah. She picked up the small brass hand bell on the side table and rang it. 'I expect you'd like tea.'

'An excellent idea.'

'Did you have time for lunch?'

'Only a snack. I spent most of the morning with Archie Clutterbuck and when I got back to the station there was plenty to do.'

'Are Prasanna and Nadar still searching for the body?'

'I fear so. Clutterbuck wasn't very happy to hear it. He doesn't think Lady Caroline or Ralph Wynne-Talbot will leave Nuala until she's found. I get the feeling he's worried about the impression William Petrie will have of his abilities.'

A servant hovered into sight and Jane ordered tea with sandwiches and cakes.

'Perhaps he doesn't understand how difficult something like this is,' she continued when the man had gone. She shuddered. 'If the body has disappeared, there could be all sorts of reasons why. Still, it's understandable not wanting to leave, especially where the lady's husband is concerned. Grieving is a long process and while there's this uncertainty, it will be hard even to begin to mourn for her.'

Tea arrived and Jane poured them both a cup. De Silva

lifted his and savoured the delicate aromas of honey and pine rising from the coppery liquid. 'Mm, white tea. This is a treat.'

'A present from Florence Clutterbuck.'

'Really?'

'Oh, not just to me. She brought gifts for everyone in the sewing circle. She wanted to thank us for all our hard work on the church kneelers. We also have some very nice soaps from Floris of London.'

'That was good of her.'

'In fact, she seems to be in a benevolent mood all round at the moment. She was full of stories about her new little dog earlier too.'

'Ah, Angel.'

'How do you know its name?'

'I met him this morning. Archie Clutterbuck was in charge of him. Which reminds me, he came out with a phrase I didn't know – *mens sana in corpore sano.*'

'It's Latin for "a healthy mind in a healthy body". It's supposed to have been said first by a Roman writer called Juvenal. It's much beloved as a motto by English public schools. But how did you come to be talking of that?'

When De Silva explained about the *Almanach de Gotha*, she laughed. 'I've heard it called the *Almanach de Gagas* too. Gaga's a rude word, it means old and not quite sane. People joke that the European aristocracy has intermarried far too often over the years and, as with animals, it breeds some unfortunate traits.'

She sipped her tea then put down the cup. 'How was Archie coping with Angel?'

'Not very well. For a small creature he's quite a handful.'

'Most small dogs tend to have an over-inflated idea of their size and importance.'

'This one certainly does.'

'I think he's at the Residence to stay, though. Florence

clearly dotes on him. Her main worry is keeping an eye on him. He sounds an adventurous little fellow and very good at getting out if he wants to go exploring. If he met a leopard, he wouldn't stand much chance, no matter how loudly he barked.'

She lifted the lid off the teapot and peered inside. 'Would you like another cup, dear? It looks a little strong but I can call for some more hot water.'

He pushed his cup towards her. 'No need, the stronger the better.'

'You still haven't told me if you found out anything interesting about Count Ranescu in the *Almanach de Gotha*.'

'I'm not sure it's fit for your ears,' he said with a grin.

'Nonsense. You know perfectly well I'm not easy to shock. Anyway, you've got me interested now, so you have to tell.'

'Clutterbuck and I strongly suspect that the lady who claims to be the countess is a fraud.'

'Goodness! What makes you think that?'

'According to the *Almanach*, and Clutterbuck says it's a recent edition, she should be sixty years old. The lady who's come to Nuala with him can't be a day over thirty-five.'

'Oh dear, if it's true, how embarrassing for them both if that becomes known. Do you need to say anything about your suspicions?'

'Quite the reverse. Archie Clutterbuck's adamant we keep them to ourselves, and I know I can rely on you to do so as well. He and William Petrie had hoped the trip to Horton Plains would provide an opportunity for putting the British government in Ranescu's good books. It seems he may be useful. Anyway, through no fault of her own, poor Mrs Wynne-Talbot threw a spanner in those works. It would be unwise to make matters worse by embarrassing the count.'

He stretched his arms above his head, laced his fingers

and yawned. 'After that delicious tea, I shall take a walk round the garden before it gets dark. Will you join me?'

'That would be nice.'

She stood up and took his arm. As they set off across the lawn, he decided not to mention that Clutterbuck was checking on Major Aubrey. There would probably be nothing suspicious in his background in any case.

CHAPTER 9

Several days elapsed before he received another summons to the Residence from Archie Clutterbuck. This time Angel was not in evidence and Darcy looked vastly more contented than he had on de Silva's previous visit.

The assistant government agent, however, was perturbed. 'You've got a nose for a mystery, de Silva, and sometimes I think it would be better if you didn't, but there it is. Colombo telegraphed. It's been two years since Major Aubrey was stationed in Calcutta and there's a gap in his record that no one seems able or willing to fill in for us.'

He frowned. 'Not long afterwards, another telegram came warning me against making any more enquiries about him.' Pausing, he took a cigarette from the box on his desk and lit it. 'So there you have it,' he said shaking out the match. 'Our choice is to accept Aubrey and his testimony at face value or challenge him. In view of the messages from Colombo, the latter would be foolhardy.'

There might be all sorts of reasons why the army didn't like to divulge what an officer had been up to, reflected de Silva. He'd noticed before that they liked to keep the stories of their black sheep quiet. It could be anything from gambling and drinking to misbehaving with a fellow officer's wife. Aubrey had been drinking early in the day when de Silva interviewed him at Horton Plains and, even though the immediate circumstances provided an excuse, he'd admitted he didn't sleep well in general. Did that indicate he had problems?

But even if he did, where did that get you? Telling Archie Clutterbuck that he, de Silva, had a vague feeling that something about Aubrey felt wrong didn't amount to a convincing argument for further investigations into Helen Wynne-Talbot's death.

'De Silva?'

'Sorry, sir. I was just thinking the situation through.'

'And your conclusion?'

De Silva took a deep breath. He was loath to give up, but for the moment it seemed the only sensible course of action. 'We accept the major's testimony,' he said reluctantly.

Clutterbuck gave him a penetrating look then nodded. 'Good, I'm glad we agree.' He flicked ash from his cigarette into an ashtray decorated with a picture of a leaping salmon. 'I suppose your search for the body still isn't getting anywhere?'

'I'm afraid not, sir.'

'How many shikaris did you send out with them?'

'Four, sir.'

Clutterbuck chewed his lower lip. 'Maybe send a few more to help.'

'Very good, sir.'

He didn't like to tell Clutterbuck that yesterday, Prasanna and Nadar had returned dejected with no news and he had given them a short respite from their arduous search. He'd have to curtail that.

'Damned difficult, I know,' the assistant government agent went on. 'But it's been a week. I have to admit, I'm beginning to wonder if it might be best if she wasn't found now. Unlikely to be a pretty sight.'

He cleared his throat. 'Well, unless there's something else you wish to discuss, I won't detain you. I'm sure you're busy and I have another meeting shortly.'

De Silva remembered his promise to Prasanna; it really was time he raised the matter. It wasn't fair to his sergeant to keep putting it off.

'There is one thing, sir.'

'Yes?' There was a touch of impatience in Clutterbuck's tone.

'My sergeant tells me he's had a complaint about the behaviour of one of the village headmen.'

'And?'

'The complaint is that the man's profiting from his position. Overcharging for government licences among other things.'

Clutterbuck looked at his watch. 'I'm sorry, de Silva, I haven't got time to go into it with you now. Telephone my secretary tomorrow. He keeps my diary and will arrange a time for us to discuss it.'

De Silva felt irritated at being put off but there was no point arguing so he nodded. Regrettably, Prasanna would have to be patient a little longer.

Clutterbuck went to his desk and took something out of a drawer. 'I almost forgot. This is a picture that was taken of our party before we went up to Horton Plains. I've no use for it and I don't suppose anyone else wants to be reminded, but it's a decent photo of Mrs Wynne-Talbot. It might be a help in your search.'

'Good idea, sir. I'll take it with me.'

CHAPTER 10

Jane was far more of a cinema fan than he was, avidly devouring all the film magazines she could lay her hands on. However, he enjoyed the visit to the cinema to see the Busby Berkley film. The choreography, with its kaleidoscopes of perfectly synchronised, tirelessly smiling bathing belles, seemed to him to have something in common with the cases he had solved over the years – a multitude of elements that eventually resolved themselves into a pattern that made sense. At least that was what you hoped would happen.

'What a delightful film,' she remarked as they drove away from the Casino cinema that evening.

'Not as much storyline as *42nd Street*, though.'

'Ah, but it's the singing and dancing one goes for.'

'I'll give you that.'

She squeezed his arm. 'Thank you for coming. They're showing *The Thin Man* next month. That will be more up your street.'

But his attention hadn't just strayed because of the film. His thoughts had distracted him too. Although he had agreed with Clutterbuck about Major Aubrey, the uncertainty he'd felt about the officer had come back to haunt him. It was hard to put the reason into words. He simply had the feeling that the dismissal of Mrs Wynne-Talbot's death as suicide was too convenient.

Then there was Ralph Wynne-Talbot. Why had he taken a provincial doctor like Hebden, whom he'd never met before, into his confidence about his wife? In a short time, they would have been in England, and able to afford the best medical help money could buy in London's famous Harley Street.

'You're very preoccupied,' said Jane as the Morris sped along the quiet roads towards Sunnybank. 'Is something wrong?'

'Not wrong exactly, but I'm concerned I've missed something.'

'You mean about Mrs Wynne-Talbot?'

'Yes. Do you remember what I told you about the count and countess?'

Jane nodded.

'It appears they're not the only people who have something to hide.'

'Really? I imagine you don't mean Archie or the Petries so that leaves Major Aubrey.'

'Precisely. I asked Clutterbuck if he would make enquiries about him. He wasn't willing at first but then he agreed to get in touch with Colombo and ask for their assistance. Clutterbuck called me up to the Residence today. Aubrey lied about being stationed in Calcutta. He hasn't been there for two years. That was strange enough but then another telegram came with instructions that there were to be no further enquiries.'

'That is odd.'

'Quite.'

'And there was no explanation?'

'None at all.'

'Does that make you suspicious of Major Aubrey? I mean as far as Mrs Wynne-Talbot's death is concerned. But then why would he want to do her harm?'

'That's what I don't know.' He paused. 'There's something

not quite right about Aubrey, quite apart from what we've heard from Colombo. When I questioned him, he seemed a troubled soul.'

'He had just witnessed a terrible death, dear.'

'Of course, but I had the feeling it was more than that.'

'How did he come to be with the hunting party?'

'Apparently, he invited himself. Archie Clutterbuck told me he let Aubrey come along because he seemed agreeable and likely to be a good shot. He talked a lot about the shooting he'd done in India and, as we know, old Archie loves a sportsman.'

Jane raised an eyebrow. 'I'm sure he does. Florence often regales us on sewing afternoons with stories of the elephant and tiger hunts he took part in when they were in Bengal. I don't think I'm the only one who finds it distasteful.'

He changed down a gear as the Morris slid into the final bend before the driveway to Sunnybank. 'I'll show you something when we get home,' he said. 'I'd be interested in your opinion.'

Settled on the floral-patterned sofa in their comfortable drawing room, de Silva dropped the photograph Clutterbuck had given him into Jane's lap. 'Here you are. Take a look and tell me what you think. Aubrey's the one on the far left.'

'So this is the rogues' gallery.' She studied the photograph in silence for a while. 'I must say, if anyone looks like a villain, it's Count Ranescu. What a belligerent-looking man! One would hesitate to argue with him.'

She tilted the photograph so that the light from the lamp on the side table fell on it more brightly. 'You know, the countess, if that's who she is, looks very familiar.'

She peered more closely at the photograph then looked up with a triumphant smile. 'I think I know who this is. When I worked in London as a governess, I had a friend who liked the theatre and sometimes we'd go to matinées together on our days off. We saw all sorts of plays – Terence Rattigan, Noel Coward, Oscar Wilde. This lady looks just like an actress who used to be in the West End. She usually played the juvenile leads, but then she ran off with a wealthy businessman and gave up the stage. The gossip columns were full of it at the time.'

De Silva rubbed his chin. 'That's most interesting. How sure are you?'

Jane looked at the photograph again. 'Pretty sure. She was a very beautiful young woman. It's hard to credit there would be anyone else who looked like her. Let me see, she would have been about twenty then. A few years younger than I was and it was fifteen years ago.' She put down the photograph. 'As you say, she looks about thirty-five, so, that would be right. Now what was her name? Laetitia...' She paused and her brow puckered. 'Laetitia Lane! That was it.'

De Silva chuckled. 'If she is an imposter, being an actress would explain how she gives such a convincing per-formance. I doubt even a genuine countess would possess more aristocratic poise.'

'I think you're rather struck with the lady.' Her smile admonished him.

'I only have eyes for you, my love.'

'I should hope so.'

She kissed his cheek. 'Seriously, if I am right, it probably makes no difference to your case. But let's just suppose that it wasn't suicide—'

'Who might be the murderer? You must have read enough detective novels to think of all the possibilities.'

She pondered a few moments. 'What if there's some-thing going on between Miss Lane and the major? Maybe it wasn't an accident that they were on the same expedition. Helen Wynne-Talbot might have overhead them talking or even discovered them together, and the major decided she must be silenced.'

'That would be a most dramatic twist, but you are making him out to be an incorrigible villain and very precipitant.'

'People can do terrible things when surprised in guilty acts, at least they do in novels.'

'Any other ideas?'

'Could Aubrey and Mrs Wynne-Talbot have rigged the whole thing? As you haven't found her body yet, how can you be sure that she's really dead? Perhaps she and the major are the ones in love and they plan to run away together.'

De Silva rubbed his chin. It was a possibility that had crossed his mind but he had dismissed it on the grounds that it would have been hard for Helen Wynne-Talbot to leave Horton Plains without attracting attention. Also, as far as he knew, Aubrey was still in Nuala. Unless he had misjudged Helen Wynne-Talbot, she didn't have the resourcefulness to go into hiding on her own until Aubrey could join her.

But then there was the missing shikari, who still wasn't accounted for. Should his absence tell them something? Might he have witnessed the incident and been bribed or threatened by Aubrey into keeping quiet? If he knew the truth of what had happened at World's End, he needed to be found, but how? His fellow shikaris were obviously not going to co-operate, either because they genuinely knew nothing about him or they too had been warned off.

His head throbbed. It was too late in the evening to sift the wheat from the... the expression refused to surface in his tired mind.

'These are interesting ideas, my love,' he said wearily. 'Unfortunately, we'll need more than inspired guesses to get to the bottom of this.' He yawned. 'I'm off to bed. Are you coming up?'

'In a moment.'

'Let me know if you think of anything else.'

'I will.'

Later, unable to sleep despite his weariness, a condition that occasionally bedevilled him, de Silva mulled over their conversation. Jane had a very good memory for names and faces and she might well be right about the countess being this Laetitia Lane woman. In that case, what were the lady's intentions? If she was the count's mistress, she wouldn't be the first woman, or the last, to snare a rich man who could give her the lifestyle she craved without being unduly concerned that he was married. It didn't inevitably mean she was a murderer.

He rolled over, glanced at the clock and groaned inwardly; it was ten past midnight. He was tempted to wake Jane and share his speculations with her but she seemed to be sound asleep and he refrained. His thoughts dwelt on Laetitia Lane. It would be interesting to know more about what she was up to. Just suppose it was more than coincidental that she and Major Aubrey were both on the Horton Plains expedition. He had to admit, his curiosity was piqued and part of him was also attracted by the possibility of scoring a point. He still couldn't shake off a lingering resentment that he had been steamrollered into abandoning any further investigation. If there was more to this business than at first met the eye, it would give him great satisfaction to show the British they were not as clever as they liked to think.

Clutterbuck had mentioned that the count and countess were staying in the guest bungalow in the Residence grounds. The guest suites in the Residence itself were given over to the Petries and Ralph Wynne-Talbot. That was very fortunate. It would be impossible to search any of the rooms in the Residence without being apprehended; there were always servants about. But if the Ranescus were out, once the servants had cleaned and tidied the rooms in the guest bungalow, it was probably left unattended for the day. Searching the bungalow was a risk, of course, Archie

Clutterbuck would explode if things went wrong, but the risk was one worth taking if a search revealed anything interesting about the countess.

The bed creaked as Jane stirred beside him. 'You're awake. Are you still thinking about your case? Have you come to any conclusions?'

He put his arms around her and kissed her. 'Sadly not. Go back to sleep, my love.'

CHAPTER 11

'Has Florence mentioned how much longer the Ranescus plan to stay in Nuala?' he asked at breakfast.

'For another week or so, I believe. She was complaining about what hard work it is entertaining them. She's quite taken to the countess whom she describes as absolutely charming, but apparently, the count is very difficult to please.' She giggled. 'In fact, the other day, Florence let her hair down in a most indiscreet way. She went so far as to call him a dreadful little man! Still, today she's arranged an early morning elephant ride and a picnic by the river before the day gets too hot. She hopes that will be a success.'

De Silva filed the information in his mind as he finished his egg hopper and wiped his lips on his napkin. Here was the perfect opportunity.

'I must be on my way.' He dropped a kiss on her cheek. 'Have a good day, my love.'

'Are you coming home for lunch?'

'No, but I'll try not to be late this evening.'

He set off in the direction of the main entrance to the Residence but then diverged onto a series of increasingly narrow roads that eventually brought him to the rear of its grounds. He had walked round them with Jane the previous year when they'd attended a garden party in the Petries' honour. Fortuitously, he had noticed where the guest bungalow was.

Moving as stealthily as a plump detective could, he went as far as the spot where the trees ended and the bungalow's lawn began. It was a pretty little place in the English style with mullioned windows and a profusion of deep pink roses growing up the whitewashed walls. He cursed inwardly at the sight of a gardener laboriously pushing a hoe back and forward in one of the flowerbeds. He looked as if he was planning to spend a long time over the task.

The door opened and a maid appeared with an armful of bedlinen. She stopped briefly to speak to the gardener and de Silva heard laughter and rapid conversation before she walked on in the direction of the main house. The gardener returned to his desultory hoeing. De Silva sighed then squatted on his haunches to watch and wait.

Nearly an hour passed before the gardener picked up his hoe and walked away. De Silva held back for a little while in case he returned, then came out of the trees and crossed the lawn to the bungalow. He had already decided that if anyone saw him, he would say there had been a report of a man acting suspiciously nearby and he had come to investigate.

He tried the door and found to his relief that the maid hadn't locked it. He pushed it open and went in. The bungalow was as pleasant inside as it was out. Pale walls made the rooms feel spacious and airy and decades of polishing had given the wooden floor a rich lustre that was set off by colourful rugs.

There wasn't a great deal of furniture in the hall or the sitting room and he soon finished his search. Moving on to the bedroom, he found a four-poster bed draped with a mosquito net; a dressing table; a chest of drawers and several cupboards. A shell-pink silk peignoir trimmed with ostrich feathers lay fanned out on the bed and dozens of expensive-looking pots and bottles containing make-up, face creams and perfume covered the dressing table. The "countess" obviously liked to be pampered.

He left the drawers until last and turned his attention to the cupboards. How Jane would have loved to look through such beautiful clothes: dresses made of fine linen, crêpe de chine and silk; immaculately tailored slacks and skirts; silk blouses and elegant hats. For the count there were shirts from Turnbull & Asser, shoes from Lobb of London and all the jackets and trousers a well-dressed man could desire.

At the bottom of one of the cupboards, he found a locked tin box that appeared to be bolted to the floor. Taking a thin piece of wire from his pocket, he started to work on the lock and after a few minutes, it clicked. He opened the lid and took careful note of how the contents were arranged before he went any further.

At first there was nothing unusual – a large wad of money; a ladies' gold dress watch; a suede pouch that contained a necklace set with diamonds; a double string of pearls and a pair of pearl earrings. The suede smelt of the same perfume that de Silva had noticed the countess wearing up at Horton Plains. At the bottom of the box he found three passports, one of them belonging to the count. De Silva opened the second one and let out a low whistle. Jane was right, it was a foreign passport with the countess's picture but the name of the holder was Laetitia Lanara. The third passport, in the same language as the count's, also had her picture but gave her name as Countess Ranescu. He wrote down some details.

When he had replaced the items as he found them, he locked the box again then started looking through the drawers in the chest and dressing table. A few minutes' search revealed nothing of interest there or in the bathroom. Last of all, he found the Ranescus' luggage stored away in a small room at the back of the bungalow.

Patiently, he checked all the trunks and cases, running his hand over their linings too. Those labelled with the count's name revealed nothing unusual, but when de Silva came to the ones that belonged to the countess, he paused at a crocodile-skin dressing case. There was a faint crackling sound when he ran his hand over the lining; something underneath it felt lumpy.

On closer inspection, he noticed that a slit had been made in the fabric then the edges had been sewn together again. He took the wire that had opened the safe and carefully unpicked the stitches. When the slit was large enough, he reached in and brought out a small packet. He was about to remove the contents when he heard a sound and froze. Was it the maid returning? Silently, he closed the dressing case, hid behind the door and waited.

Time passed very slowly. The maid, and he was fairly sure by now that it was her for she was singing a Tamil song to herself as she moved about the room, was obviously in no hurry. He heard drawers open and close and the rattle of hangers on the cupboard rails.

When at last her singing faded and the door closed, he breathed again. He must be quick; another interruption might be fatal. He peeled back the flap of the envelope and took out its contents. There were several photographs of Laetitia Lane, clearly taken by a professional photographer, and with them a letter in a language that was foreign to him. He squinted at the words and tried to make some of them out but it was no use; he would write them down and hope they meant something to Jane. He would have to ask for her help now and admit what he had been up to. He also found two more identity documents, both in languages he didn't know, and a British passport for Laetitia Lane.

The contents of the letter and details of the documents copied into his notebook, he replaced everything in the envelope and pushed it back under the lining. Now he needed to find a way of sewing the slit up. Laetitia Lane didn't look as if she spent any time on needlework, but if he was lucky, the maid might have left something useful behind.

There was nothing in the bedroom, but in the sitting room he found a small sewing basket with one of the count's shirts beside it. Quickly, he threaded a needle and went back to the store room. His stitches were clumsy, but hopefully Laetitia Lane didn't have a sharp eye for such things. He tied off the thread, restored the dressing case to the place where he had found it and went to the sitting room to replace the needle. Outside, he had just reached the trees when he heard the maid's song once more. He concealed himself behind the thick trunk of a coconut palm until she had gone into the bungalow, then he returned to the Morris.

CHAPTER 12

'The letter's written in German,' Jane said, studying the words de Silva had copied into his notebook. She was clearly enjoying having a puzzle to work out and had swiftly forgiven him for hiding his plan to search the guest bungalow from her at breakfast.

'I don't understand much of it,' she went on. 'But look.' She pointed to the first line, '*Liebling* – it means darling – and this word, *gefahr*, is danger. Then here,' she indicated another line, 'I think it says "I have sent money there for you".'

She scanned the rest of the letter. 'That's all I can make out, except this part at the end. It looks like an address but not one here in Ceylon. As for the passports, the one in the name of Laetitia Lanara is Italian. The other two are French and German.'

'Well, it's a start.'

'What do you think this is all about, Shanti? Is there more to Laetitia Lane than simply being the count's mistress? Why else would she need all these identities?'

'She's up to something, I'm sure, and I'd like to know what, but I may come up against some opposition from Archie Clutterbuck.'

'Why? If Miss Lane is doing something she shouldn't, won't he want to know?'

'In theory, yes. He told me that the British are worried about Germany taking an interest in Romania.'

'Why would they do that?'

'Because Romania has oil and an arms industry, both of which might be very useful to the Germans.'

Jane shivered. 'When the Great War came to an end, people said it was the war to end all wars. It's dreadful to think they might be proved wrong. If you think Laetitia Lane's spying for the Germans and trying to work her way into Count Ranescu's confidence, you ought to tell Archie Clutterbuck.'

'Oh, I will.' He hesitated to admit to Jane how much he would enjoy stealing a march on the assistant government agent, even if it might prove a little tricky explaining why he had searched the guest bungalow in the first place.

'Perhaps she and Major Aubrey are in league,' Jane mused.

'Both spies? This really is beginning to sound like the plot for a film or a novel.'

'It would make an exciting one, I'm sure. But it is rather far-fetched to assume that either of them had a hand in Helen Wynne-Talbot's death.'

'I expect you're right.' He looked up at the sun. 'The picnic's probably finished by now but I think I'll leave asking to see Clutterbuck for the moment. I'd like a bit of time to mull over how to present my findings to him.'

He stood up. 'I'll pay a quick visit to the station and see what's going on down there. In any case, Clutterbuck will want to know how the search for Helen Wynne-Talbot's body is going. Unfortunately, I doubt I'll have much news for him. If she really did fall, finding her in the jungle will be like looking for a needle in a haystack.'

Jane shuddered. 'That poor husband of hers, one can hardly comprehend how he must be feeling.'

'I sincerely hope I never have to find out first-hand.'

'That's very unlikely, dear. I prefer to admire the view at World's End from a safe distance.'

'Well, I'll be off. I'll try not to be long. Would you like to go out this evening?'

'There's nothing on at the Casino but I believe the Crown Hotel has a trio playing after dinner and there will be dancing.'

'Would you like that?'

'Yes, I think I would. We haven't been dancing for a long time.'

'Then let's do it.'

He took her hand, pulled her out of her chair and bowed. 'May I have this dance, ma'am?'

'Certainly, you may, sir.'

Laughing, they twirled around the room until they had to stop to catch their breath. 'I'm not as fit as I was,' he said ruefully.

'Nor am I, but never mind.' She kissed his cheek. 'Now, off you go. I'll tell Cook to serve dinner a little earlier than usual so we have a nice long evening afterwards. Even if we can't dance the night away anymore, we can still enjoy the music.'

* * *

Nuala's streets drowsed in the afternoon heat. Even in the bazaar, activity had slowed to a lethargic pace. A lone bullock pulled at a wilting bundle of coriander on one of the stalls, but the old woman behind the counter just flapped her hands half-heartedly in its direction and retreated to the shade. Even the children had given up playing. Stretched out on the parched ground, dogs twitched in their sleep.

A girl in a yellow sari who seemed livelier than the rest attracted his attention. He slowed and waved her across the road. As he did so, he glimpsed a pair of beautiful eyes above the veil she had drawn across her face to keep out the dust.

The sight of her reminded him yet again that Prasanna was still waiting for help with – what was the girl's name? Kuveni – that was it. A shame that developments meant that, once again, tomorrow probably wasn't going to be a good time to raise the issue. The girl reached the other side of the road and disappeared into a narrow alley. How gracefully she walked, yet her sari looked old and shabby. He wondered who she was.

The clock on the post office's tower struck four as he parked the Morris along the side wall of the police station where there was some shade. Speculating as to whether Nadar would be asleep or awake, he went inside, letting the front door bang as he closed it. His constable jumped to his feet, quickly fastening the top button of his tunic. De Silva suppressed a smile as the young man drew himself up like a ramrod and assumed an expression of the utmost gravity.

'Good afternoon, Inspector.'

De Silva nodded. 'On your own, I see. Where's Prasanna?'

'He's just gone out for a while, sir.'

'Anything to report?'

'There was a telephone call at ten o'clock from a gentleman who wanted to speak to you but he wouldn't give his name.'

'So how am I supposed to ring him back?'

'He said he would call again, sir, but he has not yet done so.'

'Did he say what he wanted, this mystery man?'

'He said he needed to speak to you on a very important matter concerning Mrs Wynne-Talbot.'

De Silva's brow puckered. When he had worked in the police force in Colombo, it had been a not-infrequent occurrence to find people coming into the station claiming that they had vital information about one of the crimes the police were trying to solve. Most of them had been cranks, particularly the ones who would not give their names. He'd soon learnt to season their "vital information" with a generous pinch of salt.

'If he calls again, Nadar, tell him I want his name, and details of how to contact him before anything else.'

Nadar looked a little crestfallen. 'Yes, Inspector.'

'Never mind, Nadar, I'm not blaming you. How is the baby by the way? Sleeping better, I hope?'

The constable's plump countenance brightened. 'He is, thank you, sir. Two teeth have arrived and he is much happier than he was. My wife and I also.'

'That's excellent news. I hope it lasts.'

'Thank you, sir.'

So, no more dormouse, at least for the moment, de Silva thought. He made a telephone call to the Residence and, after a short wait, was told Clutterbuck would be free to see him at eleven the next morning. He hesitated, it was sooner than expected and he had planned to take a little longer composing his speech; on the other hand, it would be a load off his mind. He was also aware that he owed it to Prasanna to try to make some progress with his lady friend's problem.

'Thank you,' he said. 'Tell him I will be there.'

He stood up and went to the small mirror over the washbasin in the corner of his office. His reflection stared back at him resolutely. He straightened his badge and stood there for a few moments, then, humming the tune from *42nd Street*, he went out to the Morris and drove home in the sunshine.

CHAPTER 13

While he shaved, he whistled one of the tunes he and Jane had danced to the previous night.

'It's good to see you so cheerful,' she remarked, coming into the room. 'Wasn't it a lovely evening? That pianist played beautifully and the singer and the bass player did very well too. I hope the Crown make a regular feature of having them perform.'

'Yes, it would be nice if they did. If I may say so, my wife was the best dancer there.'

Jane laughed. 'Oh, what nonsense. There were lots of women who danced far better than I ever could.'

He scraped away the last of the shaving foam and patted his cheeks dry. 'I disagree entirely.'

'That's very sweet of you, dear.' She looked wistful. 'But it was so nice to hear some music. I've missed that.'

'But what about Florence's musical soirées? I thought you enjoyed those.'

'Oh I do, but I love to hear modern music too, the kind one dances to.'

He hung up his towel. 'I enjoyed it as well. If there's a chance, we'll go again.'

On the way to the station, an idea crossed his mind. He'd have to give it some thought, but for now, he must concentrate on the interview with Archie Clutterbuck.

At the station, Nadar looked rather more rumpled than

he had the previous day. Presumably another baby tooth loomed: dormouse time again. More in hope than anticipation, he left instructions for tasks to be done that day and set off.

The road leading to the Residence was busy with traffic coming in from the countryside: bullock carts laden with boxes of vegetables, bananas, mangoes and other fruits, as well as great leafy bundles of herbs. Rickshaws and bicycles jostled for space too.

As the gates came into sight, de Silva suffered a momentary pang of doubt. He hoped he wasn't going to stir up a hornets' nest without good cause. His foot eased off the accelerator but then he pulled himself together again. What he had found at the guest bungalow could be important. If it was, it ought to improve his standing with the British rather than diminish it. As for Prasanna, he was a reliable young man and his information must be given due weight. If there was any truth in the allegations against the headman, the British, with their much-vaunted sense of fair play, could hardly complain. And if there wasn't, it was still fair that the matter was looked into.

To the right-hand side of the drive, the Residence's gardeners were trimming the edges of the lawns and hoeing already immaculate flowerbeds filled with roses, marigolds and geraniums. The style was very formal, de Silva reflected. In his own garden, he preferred a touch of natural wildness. According to Jane, however, the Residence garden was a prime example of British taste.

He met Florence on the front steps, the little black and white household mop cavorting at her heels.

'Good morning, ma'am.'

'Inspector de Silva! Good morning to you too. Angel and I are about to go for a walk around the grounds.'

The little dog puffed out his chest and emitted a high-pitched bark then stopped to sniff at de Silva's trouser leg.

Florence beamed. 'Ah look, he likes you. He's such a dear little chap.'

'He certainly is, ma'am,' said de Silva, relieved not to have his ankles nipped or worse.

'I do hope your wife is well?'

'Very well, thank you, ma'am.'

'Unfortunately, with our guests here, there hasn't been much time for my usual activities, so I've not seen my friends as often as I would like.'

'I'm sure you are greatly missed, ma'am.'

'One hopes so. Well, I mustn't keep you, Inspector. Come along, Angel.'

'Enjoy your walk, ma'am.'

'Thank you, I'm sure we shall.'

Perhaps, she wasn't such a bad sort after all, thought de Silva as Florence trotted away with her shaggy companion. There must be times when her position in life wasn't easy. From what Jane had told him, the present was one of those times, obliged to entertain a guest whom she found extremely uncongenial.

He straightened his collar and put his hand on the bell pull beside the front door. There was a jangling sound inside the house and a moment later, a servant appeared. Ushered into the study, he found Clutterbuck at his desk with Darcy snoozing at his feet.

The assistant government agent put the cap back on his pen and closed the ledger in which he had been writing. 'Ah, de Silva! Another fine morning, eh? We shall miss this spell when the monsoon comes next month. At least the rain is warmer than it is at home.'

'So my wife tells me, sir.'

Darcy hauled himself up from the rug and ambled round the desk to have his ears scratched. 'The poor old chap's glad to have a bit of peace,' said Clutterbuck. 'My wife and her little blighter have gone for a walk.'

'Yes, I met them on the way out.'

'So, do you have news about the whereabouts of the late Mrs Wynne-Talbot?'

'I'm afraid not, sir. I wanted to speak to you on another matter.'

Clutterbuck leant back in his chair. 'Something I'll want to hear, I hope.'

De Silva paused. The exact wording of the speech he had rehearsed so carefully after he'd woken at dawn deserted him; he would have to improvise.

'I have some information about the Ranescus.'

Clutterbuck looked irritable. 'I told you matters are sensitive where the count's concerned,' he growled. 'I thought you could be trusted to use your common sense.' A low rumble broke from Darcy's throat. He rolled over and raised his head. De Silva ignored his owner's implicit slur and ploughed on.

'I believe that what I found will be of interest to you.'

'I'm listening.'

De Silva drew a deep breath. 'I found an opportunity to search the guest bungalow here when the count and countess were at the elephant hunt and picnic.'

A thunderous expression came over Clutterbuck's face; he struck the desk with a clenched fist. 'You did what? Goddammit man, do you want to ruin what little's left of our good relations with the count? What on earth possessed you?'

'Hear me out, sir. I think you will be interested in what I discovered.'

'It had better be good!'

'I showed my wife the photograph you gave me of your hunting party up at the Plains. Jane was sure she recognised the countess. She was convinced the lady is English and a former actress who used to appear on the London stage.'

'What of it? We'd already reached the conclusion she

may be the count's mistress, not his wife. Is her history relevant? In any case, with great respect to Mrs de Silva, she may be wrong.'

'I think not, sir. The countess possesses a passport that shows her to be Italian as she claims to be, but I found others, one of them a British passport in the name of Laetitia Lane – the name my wife recalled.'

He pulled his notebook from his breast pocket and pushed it across the desk. 'This is the text of a letter I also found hidden in a piece of Miss Lane's luggage.'

Frowning, the assistant government agent scanned the words de Silva had copied out.

'You mentioned Germany's interest in Romania,' ventured de Silva. 'My wife believes this letter is written in German and, in addition to that, one of the passports is for a German national.'

Clutterbuck's frown deepened. 'An Englishwoman working against her country's interests?' He opened his top drawer and dropped de Silva's notebook on top of the papers it contained. 'You'll say no more about this, de Silva. It's way out of your league. If there's any truth in the allegation, William Petrie and I will take charge. Is that understood?'

De Silva felt nettled. Clutterbuck wouldn't even have the information if it wasn't for him.

'I said, is that understood?'

'Understood.' De Silva left a barely perceptible pause before adding, 'sir.'

'You're sure no one saw you go in or out of the guest bungalow?'

'Yes.'

'At least that's something to be grateful for.' He closed the top drawer firmly. 'Well, you can get off now, but remember, where this Wynne-Talbot business is concerned, no more snooping around. Just find the body so the husband can bury her.'

* * *

The Morris protested as he slammed the gearstick into second and pressed down hard on the accelerator to turn out of the Residence's drive. Snooping around indeed. It was the same old story with the British; it had happened more than once when he was with the Colombo force. They were happy to use his services when it suited them but the moment it didn't, they treated him like some seedy private detective.

At home, lunch waited for him but he was too preoccupied to take much notice of what he ate.

Jane looked at him worriedly. 'Did it go badly with Archie Clutterbuck?'

He grunted and pushed his plate away unfinished. 'You could say that.'

'So you don't think he'll investigate Laetitia Lane?'

'I've no idea what he'll do,' de Silva snapped. 'I've been warned off the whole matter.'

'Oh, Shanti, I'm sorry. I know it's hard sometimes and you're upset.'

'Upset? I'm not upset. That fool Clutterbuck can do as he likes. I wash my hands of it!'

Jane raised a quizzical eyebrow. Contrition overcame de Silva.

'Well, perhaps I am just a bit upset. But more than that, I'm angry.'

She came round to his side of the table and kissed his cheek. 'I understand. Really I do.'

He sighed. 'It's at times like these that I have to remind myself that if the British were not in Ceylon, we might never have met.'

'I hope that's comfort enough.'

He took her hand to his lips and kissed it. 'You know it is.' He paused then groaned. 'Poor Prasanna, I didn't even get as far as talking to Clutterbuck about this headman again and goodness knows when I will. Not while Clutterbuck and I are at odds anyway.'

'What problem does Prasanna have?' Jane went back to her seat. 'You haven't mentioned anything up until now.'

'How shameful of this man,' she said when he had explained about Kuveni and her family.

'If there's truth in it, yes, it's a serious breach of the trust that has been placed in him. But we mustn't ignore the possibility that when a pretty girl meets an impressionable young man, she might be tempted to take advantage and exaggerate her family's plight. Before we can take matters any further, Clutterbuck would need to have the records examined to see how this headman has been discharging his duties. If there are any suspicions of wrongdoing, I was hoping he would agree to make an official inspection.'

'I expect he'll calm down in a few days.'

'I hope so.'

'Oh, of course he will and then you can talk to him. Poor Sergeant Prasanna. We must do whatever we can to help. He's obviously very fond of this girl, but if she's from one of the villages, his mother might not think her suitable. That will mean problems that we of all people should sympathise with.'

'That's true.'

'Are you going back to the station this afternoon?'

'I ought to for an hour or so. I'd better send Prasanna out again for another try, although the chances of finding Helen Wynne-Talbot are looking pretty slim. He can take a few extra shikaris with him this time. They might be more help than young Nadar. Then I'll come home and spend some time in the garden.'

'Excellent, that will cheer you up.'

'It usually does. That and the company of my lovely wife.' He pushed his chair away from the table and stood up reluctantly. 'I'll be on my way.' He sighed. 'I think Nadar's baby is teething again. It's not ideal leaving him in charge but what else can I do? Calling Prasanna off the search too would amount to admitting defeat.'

Jane looked sad. 'But it may be what has to be done.'

'That is for Archie Clutterbuck to decide.'

Impulsively, she reached across the table and squeezed his hand. 'I'm glad you see it that way.'

The Morris waited for him on the drive. The comforting smell of leather met him as he eased into the seat and, by the time he arrived, he was in better humour. Far from being asleep, Nadar was busy with the tasks he had been given that morning and seemed to be making a good job of them. He was palpably relieved at the news that he was not required to return to the search for Helen Wynne-Talbot.

Sergeant Prasanna was less happy. As he went off gloomily to hire more shikaris, de Silva wondered whether it was time to consider taking over the search himself.

CHAPTER 14

Early the following morning, he was sitting at his desk when the telephone rang. To his surprise, he heard a familiar gruff voice at the other end of the line.

'De Silva? Archie Clutterbuck here.' There was a pause and the clearing of a throat. 'De Silva? Are you there?'

'Yes, sir.' He waited. Clearly something was coming that was going to cost the assistant government agent a considerable effort.

'De Silva, it seems I owe you an apology.' Another pause. 'I was too hasty yesterday. The thing is, it's not been an easy week. The Powers that Be have been coming down on Petrie wanting to know what progress we're making with this Ranescu fellow and that comes back on me. So far, they're not happy with what we have to tell them. The hunting expedition was a fiasco and then your news about the countess. De Silva, can you hear me?'

De Silva smiled to himself. Poor old Archie. It can't have been easy for him to admit he was in the wrong, even if he tempered his admission by putting some of the blame on Petrie and those mysterious powers.

'Yes, sir, and I accept your apology with thanks. Most generous of you.'

'Good man, knew I could rely on you. Now, we have another problem. That damned fellow Ranescu! He's nothing but a magnet for trouble. The Lane woman, if that's really her name, told him she wasn't well and needed to sleep alone. When he woke in the morning, he found she'd done a bunk. He claims she's taken some very valuable jewellery with her.'

De Silva's eyes widened. 'Is he still claiming she's his wife?'

'Not anymore. He admits now that they met at the gambling tables in Monaco.'

De Silva thought quickly. 'Unless she has access to a car, the train from Nanu Oya is the only way for her to get down to Kandy.' He looked at his watch. 'I should have just enough time to get to the station before today's train leaves.'

'Then get on with it and catch up with her, de Silva. If she gets to Kandy before we find her, she may give us the slip entirely. If we fall at this fence, and Ranescu loses money, it may be the final straw that sets him against us once and for all, and I don't want to take the blame.'

'Understood, sir. I'm on my way.'

Rummaging in one of his desk drawers, he found the photograph of the hunting party then went to the cupboard where he kept a spare set of civilian clothes. Swiftly, he changed his uniform for a sarong and a loose cotton tunic, putting his police badge in the breast pocket. If he caught up with Laetitia Lane on her way to Kandy, rather than apprehending her straight away, it would be interesting to follow to see where she went.

At the door, he looked back. Who knew how this would end? He returned to his desk, buckled his holster on under the tunic and tucked his Webley into it.

* * *

Luckily, there wasn't much traffic on the road to Nanu Oya and he reached the station shortly before the train was due to depart. He hurried to the ticket office and showed the photograph to the clerk.

'Have any of these people bought a ticket for the train to Kandy this morning?'

The man peered at the faces in the photograph for a few moments then shook his head. 'No, no one of that appearance has been here today.'

'And you're the only one selling tickets?'

'Yes, but it is possible that some of the passengers send servants from their houses or hotels to purchase tickets for them. When I am busy here, I do not see everyone who boards the train.'

De Silva heard ominous hooting coming from the platform. Dismayed, he realised that in his haste he had brought very little money with him. He dug into his breast pocket and produced his badge. 'Give me a ticket to Kandy. First Class. You'll be paid later.'

A look of alarm came over the clerk's face. 'Sir, I cannot—'

'Inspector,' de Silva said firmly. 'I am Inspector de Silva of the Nuala police and if you don't issue that ticket in the next ten seconds, the government agent will want to know why.'

The clerk's hand shook as he wrote out the ticket. With mounting irritation, de Silva watched the slow, looping writing cross the paper. Another burst of hooting came from the platform and he snatched the ticket from the counter and dashed to the gate, ignoring the guard who tried to stop him. A moment later, he wrenched open the nearest door and jumped aboard. With a final blast, the train jolted forward and started to rumble down the line.

He stood at the entrance to the carriage's corridor and waited for his laboured breathing to subside. His heart thumped and flecks of red and green danced before his eyes. Jane would tell him he was getting too old for this kind of escapade. She might be right.

When he recovered, he walked back to the head of the train and started to comb the carriages one by one. Third Class was the hardest to search, the carriages were so full of people, baskets, bags, boxes, even goats and squawking cages of hens. He moved on to Second Class and drew a similar blank. Initially, he had guessed that if Laetitia Lane was trying to escape on the train, she would choose one of the more crowded carriages to hide in, but perhaps he was wrong. Maybe a woman like her would simply travel First Class and defy anyone to see through whatever disguise she decided to adopt.

Cautiously, he entered that part of the train and stopped at the first door he came to. The compartment's occupants were an elderly couple in western dress. Neither of them bothered to look up from their books as he passed. The next four compartments were similarly unfruitful but at the sixth, he paused, hanging back a little so as not to attract the attention of the woman inside. Dressed in the white habit of a nun, she was sitting in one of the window seats, her eyes downcast as she studied the book in her lap. As she read, her long, slim fingers counted the beads of a rosary.

His heartbeat quickened. There was something suspiciously serene about this woman. He very much suspected she was his quarry. It was worth checking the final compartments, however; there was plenty of time before the first stop. Even if she decided to get off then, he would be back in time to see her go.

He waited until the train entered a tunnel then crept past the door while the corridor was in semi-darkness. When the train emerged into the open air once more, he continued his search, but none of the remaining compartments had anyone in them who could by any stretch of the imagination be Laetitia Lane. He returned to the carriage next to the nun's and sat down to wait for their arrival in Kandy.

The journey down to the city seemed interminable. At each halt, he went to the door of his compartment and listened intently but the nun stayed where she was. All he could hear was the faint click of the rosary beads. Breakfast seemed a long time ago but he bought sparingly from the food vendors who came past. At Kandy, the nun would probably take a rickshaw to her destination and he needed to have the means to follow her. An argument with a rickshaw driver was likely to attract attention and he'd seen crowds set on people who tried to avoid the fare.

At last the train arrived into Kandy station and halted with a great belch of steam. Guards walked along the platform banging open the doors, and porters hurried to take passengers' luggage. De Silva disembarked and concealed himself near a group of them until he saw the nun climb down from the train. He studied her intently; her wimple and the cowl of the travelling cloak she wore made it hard to see much of her face, but the height and build seemed right for Laetitia Lane. Surely there was a good chance this was her? If it wasn't and the real Laetitia Lane had escaped, he would feel the failure keenly, even if others excused it.

She summoned a porter and pointed to the compartment where she had been sitting. The man bounded up the steps and returned a moment later with a leather suitcase and a small travelling bag. De Silva wondered if either of them contained the jewellery. Or would Laetitia Lane take the precaution of concealing it about her person? If it was her, she had discarded the distinctive crocodile-skin dressing case.

Her small amount of luggage assembled, the nun followed the porter out of the station and de Silva followed them. Dozens of rickshaws waited in the forecourt beyond the station's curved, modern façade, their drivers competing for trade with the hawkers trying to sell the arrivals food and offerings of flowers for Kandy's famous temple.

At one point, he was afraid he would lose sight of his quarry, then, to his relief, he saw her stop beside a rickshaw and speak to the driver. As the porter loaded her luggage and she stepped into the cab, de Silva beckoned to the driver of another rickshaw that waited nearby and told him to tail them. The man looked uncertain but the flash of a few rupee coins brought a smile to his face. De Silva only hoped the journey wouldn't be longer than he could pay for.

The rickshaw set off in the direction of the Kiri Muhuda, Kandy's great lake. Its other name was the Sea of Milk and under different circumstances, de Silva would have enjoyed revisiting its sparking waters and the beautiful balustrades and shady promenades that surrounded them, but for the present, his attention was focused on the shrouded figure jolting along in the rickshaw ahead of him. His stomach tightened.

The rickshaw turned onto the road along the north shore and the dazzling golden bulk of the Temple of the Tooth reared up in front of him. Tangerine-robed monks and worshippers bearing offerings of flowers passed up and down the broad steps to the great entrance, insignificant as worker ants in the face of the temple's magnificence. He wiped his brow, wishing he could go inside that vast, cool space and let it calm the jangling in his brain, but of course that was impossible.

Ahead of him, the rickshaw left the lakeshore and threaded its way into the streets behind the temple. At last it halted at a whitewashed house next to a small chapel. The knot in de Silva's stomach pinched tighter; in a few moments, he would know whether he was right or wrong.

He rapped on the partition separating him from his driver and told the man to pass the house then stop around the corner. There, climbing down, he parted with some of his small supply of money and returned to the chapel end of the street. He was just in time to see the door of the house open and the nun step inside.

The street was deserted now except for a small black cat curled up asleep in a patch of shade by the chapel wall. Someone had planted yellow and orange marigolds in a terracotta pot by the door to the house; the scene was a picture of drowsy peace. Doubt crept into his mind, but he must go on. It was better to look a fool than allow his quarry to escape. His hand felt for the reassurance of his gun, although, in the circumstances, he felt sacrilegious having it.

As he walked towards the house, the door opened again and a different nun emerged carrying a small tin bowl. He stopped and watched her stoop to put it down in the shade.

The cat looked up at the clink of metal on stone. It stretched, then stood up and arched its back before going to rub up against the nun's knees. She bent to stroke its head and it started to lap at the milk. She waited until it was all gone then picked up the bowl. After a last fondle for the cat, she turned to go back inside then stopped. Glancing at de Silva, she smiled. 'May I help you?' she asked in English.

He drew a deep breath. 'The lady who just returned from Nanu Oya, does she live here?'

The nun looked surprised. 'Sister Honoria? Why yes. She's lived here for many years, but she has spent the last few days at our sister mission in the hill country. Would you like to speak to her? Do you wish me to call her?'

De Silva hesitated. It was dawning on him that the nun he had followed wasn't Laetitia Lane. In his eagerness, he had been too ready to assume she would take the first available train out of Nanu Oya. Instead, she might be anywhere by now.

The door opened and a face appeared. 'Sister Barbara? Is something the matter?'

'Ah, here she is,' said the first nun. 'Sister Honoria, this gentleman is asking for you.'

De Silva took in the gentle expression in the grey eyes;

the slightly crooked teeth revealed by a sweet smile and the retroussé nose. This was not Laetitia Lane. He flushed. 'Forgive me, ma'am. A mistake. I thought you were someone else.'

'It's very warm today,' Sister Honoria said kindly. 'May we offer you something cool to drink?'

Stammering his excuses, de Silva bowed and hurried away. He didn't want to have to answer any questions. The knot in his stomach was replaced by a dull ache. The journey had been a waste of time. Now he had to get home with almost no money and he was hot and hungry into the bargain. Part of him wished he had accepted the nun's offer after all.

When he'd counted his remaining coins, he decided to save them for food and drink and walk to the station. The train back to Nanu Oya would have departed anyway. He would have to sleep at the station that night. Hopefully there would be a spare bench in the waiting room where he could stretch out.

He felt a pang of guilt; Jane would worry and he didn't want that. After a few moments' thought, the best solution he came up with was to go to the Kandy police and enlist their help. They must have a telephone he could call Jane from. No doubt they would enjoy a few jokes at the expense of a stranded provincial policeman but he would have to put up with that.

CHAPTER 15

'It's a relief to have you back safely,' said Jane when he arrived home late the following day. The Sunday train up from Kandy was a slow one in any case and there had been several delays for everything from goats to fallen branches on the line. 'But I wish you'd told me where you were a bit sooner,' she added.

'I know, I'm sorry. After Archie Clutterbuck told me Miss Lane had made a run for it, I didn't want to risk delaying, however briefly.'

'I suppose I forgive you.' Jane smiled. 'Anyway, I'm very glad you've made things up with Archie.'

'He made things up with me. He has given me an apology.'

'So he bloody well should. Now, if you had so little money left to buy food, you must be ravenous.'

'I am rather hungry.'

'I'll tell Cook to have dinner ready in half an hour.'

'Good, that will give me time to wash and change my clothes.'

* * *

'So, I am out of ideas,' he said, as he tucked into a large bowl of rice with dahl and curry. 'Laetitia Lane may be any of a hundred places. My journey to Kandy was a wild duck hunt.'

'A wild goose chase, dear.'

'Hmm.' He understood that the governess in his wife found it hard to shake off the habit, but there were times when he found her linguistic policing somewhat trying.

She pondered for a few moments. 'If she wasn't on the train,' she resumed, 'isn't it possible that she's still in Nuala? Often the best hiding place is the one people least expect. We tend to think that someone who's trying to escape will get as far away as possible but it isn't necessarily the case.'

He nodded reluctantly, wishing he had thought of that himself. 'You have a point. I suppose Nadar and I could search the town for a day, but I'd be surprised if she doesn't leave eventually. Why would she stay, except perhaps with the idea of letting the fuss die down? After all, she can hardly sell all the jewels in Nuala. If they are of the high quality and value that Ranescu claims, it would cause a great deal of comment.'

'She might offer them to a jeweller who's less than scrupulous and asks no questions.'

De Silva shook his head. 'There's no one in Nuala who deals in expensive stones. The only jewellery you find up here is in the bazaar and most of that is cheap trinkets. No, if Ranescu's telling the truth and Miss Lane wants the best price for her ill-gotten gains, she will need to be in Kandy or, better still, Colombo.'

'I wonder if she really has stolen them.'

'What makes you doubt it?'

'Florence is very suspicious about whether the count is telling the truth and she may be right to mistrust him.' She shrugged. 'But then one must make allowances for the fact that she dislikes him intensely.' Her eyes twinkled. 'He had the temerity to call Angel an annoying little creature and she heard the remark.'

'Ah, that would be enough to banish him from her good books forever.'

'Absolutely.'

De Silva mopped up the last of the spicy sauce on his plate. 'That was delicious. Well, if Nadar and I are to have any success with this search, I suppose we shall have to get on with it, but it's late and I deserve a rest so it will have to wait until morning.'

'What about Sergeant Prasanna?'

'He's still looking for the body. A shame as he might be more useful here, but Nadar tries his best and the experience will be good practice for him.'

'So what will you do?'

'I'll have to check at the station before the train leaves tomorrow morning in case Miss Lane does try to escape that way. I think it's more likely she will. She'll need to have found a car and chauffeur to take her to Nanu Oya, but it's not far and many people travel there. It will be much less conspicuous than arranging for someone to drive her all the way down to Kandy. A booking for that is far more likely to be remarked on and she will expect us to be checking with the hotels that provide chauffeur services. There's only Nadar and myself to do it but we can use the telephone. We may as well search the bazaar as well. She might need money and be trying to sell some of the less-valuable pieces of jewellery there.'

'Poor Ralph Wynne-Talbot. It must be very hard for him having to wait like this. I hear from Florence that Lady Caroline is terribly anxious about him.'

'Let's hope he doesn't have to wait much longer.'

'What happens if you never find the body?'

'Mrs Wynne-Talbot will have to be declared missing, presumed dead. Not a very satisfactory outcome.'

'If I were in Ralph Wynne-Talbot's place, I think I would find it even worse never to know what happened to my wife. None of us want to be the one left behind, but at least a funeral is a fitting way of taking the first steps towards coming to terms with one's grief.'

He squeezed her shoulder. 'Goodness, this conversation has taken a very solemn turn. We need to go dancing again to cheer ourselves up.'

'Indeed we do, but all the same the poor man's predicament reminds me how lucky I am to have you.'

He gave her a mischievous smile. 'I'm glad you appreciate it.' Yawning, he got to his feet. 'I think I'll have an early night. That bench at the train station was as hard as granite.' He rubbed the small of his back. 'Next time, Count Ranescu can do his own chasing after his lady friend.'

CHAPTER 16

The next morning, de Silva called in briefly at the police station to explain the situation to Nadar. He left him telephoning hotels and set off for Nanu Oya, but no one resembling Laetitia Lane took the Kandy train.

He beat an irritable tattoo on the Morris's steering wheel as he drove back to Nuala. His resources were far too slim; it was very likely this woman would give them the slip but what could he do about it?

At the station, Nadar was just replacing the receiver.

'Anything to report, Constable?'

'I'm afraid not, sir. But the gentleman who wanted to speak to you on Thursday telephoned again. He still wouldn't leave his name.'

'Well, I certainly haven't time to waste on him now. You'd better go home and change into some clothes that will make you less conspicuous. I want to make a search of the bazaar and we mustn't draw attention to ourselves.'

'Yes, sir.'

'When you come back, I'll show you a photograph of Miss Lane. She may have adopted some sort of disguise but it should help us a little.'

While Nadar was gone, de Silva changed into the traditional clothing he had snatched up before he left home and also fashioned the length of cloth he had brought with him into a turban. It wasn't much of a disguise and Laetitia

Lane had seen him at close quarters but he would have to rely on the British tendency to fail to distinguish between one Ceylonese face and another. For once, it might be something to be thankful for.

Nadar returned and, in silence at first, they walked briskly in the direction of the bazaar.

It was busy with the start of the week's trading but no suspicious sights met their eyes. After wandering around for a while observing passers-by, de Silva decided they should go their separate ways and sent Nadar to try the lake area while he took the town streets.

Outside the cinema, people studied the posters for forthcoming films. Others browsed the windows of shops or went in and out of the numerous guest houses that had sprung up in Nuala to serve the needs of the summer tourists in search of the hills' cooler climate. Some drank tea or ate cakes and sweetmeats at street cafés.

The area of Nuala where he had started his search didn't attract many British. Most people were Sinhalese or Tamil, but there were a number of Arabs, probably the merchants who liked to come to Nuala to do business. Out of the corner of his eye, de Silva noticed one particularly tall man dressed in a black robe and a dark turban. He was heavily bearded and his eyes glittered in his dark-skinned face; the traditional curved dagger gleamed in his belt. A few paces behind him, a heavily veiled woman, presumably his wife, followed with her head meekly bowed.

The couple appeared to be on their way to a nearby guest house and, as the man passed him and turned to go through the doors, de Silva smelt a whiff of something like axle grease. He stopped and waited for the lady to follow and it was then that another scent invaded his nostrils: a luxurious, elegant, expensive aroma. This wasn't something the lady had bought in the bazaar. Unmistakably, it was French perfume.

He took note of the name of the guest house and hurried back to the station. He had told Nadar to meet him there before dark and the constable wasn't far behind. The more he thought about the Arab and his wife, the more de Silva's spirits lifted. Perhaps he was really onto something this time. And if the dutiful-looking wife was Laetitia Lane, who was her companion? Was he the writer of that impenetrable letter he had found at the bungalow?

The brief tropical dusk had turned to night by the time he and Nadar reached the guest house. De Silva had changed back into uniform; he wore the holster containing his gun and had made sure the Webley was loaded. The owner of the guest house gave his badge a wary look when he demanded to know which room the Arab and his wife were staying in.

'Number two,' the man said nervously. 'But I know nothing about them, just that they will stay three nights, perhaps longer. The man has paid the first of the money already.'

'Have they ordered food?'

The owner nodded. 'I must have it brought to their room.'

'We will wait until it's ready, then you must show us the way.'

'But, sir—'

'No arguments. Once you've knocked on the door, you will leave everything else to us.'

The food ready, the owner led them up the stairs to the second floor. He stopped at a door decorated with a lopsided metal '2', and knocked.

'Yes?' shouted a male voice in Tamil.

'The food is here, sir.'

'Leave it outside the door. I'll collect it in a moment.'

De Silva put a finger to his lips and nodded.

'Yes, sir,' the man replied. He put the tray on the floor

and moved away down the stairs as de Silva indicated.

De Silva positioned himself to one side of the door and motioned Nadar to stand behind him. He cocked his gun and listened intently as footsteps approached.

Laetitia Lane's eyes widened. She tried to slam the door in his face but he wedged his foot in the way. Behind her, he saw Major Aubrey drop the cloth that was in his hand and lunge for the table where the curved dagger lay. He had removed his turban and robe along with the beard and now wore only a pair of trousers. Traces of dark-brown greasepaint streaked his face.

De Silva took aim and fired and the dagger spun off the table and flew across the floor. With unexpected presence of mind, Nadar ran over and seized it while Aubrey caught his foot on the edge of a rug and crashed to the floor. The smell of cordite filled the room and de Silva's ears rang. He hadn't fired a gun since his Colombo days.

As the reverberations died away, Laetitia Lane was the first to recover. She had removed her burka and wore a loose silk robe. There was no disputing that it was her.

'Why, Inspector de Silva!' she said coolly. 'Forgive us for receiving you in such an unfriendly fashion. We weren't expecting company but, now you're here, won't you join us for dinner?'

CHAPTER 17

Aubrey regained his feet and de Silva noticed that the skin on his chest bore several scars that looked fairly recent. He picked up a shirt and pulled it on. When he spoke, his tone was more hostile than his companion's.

'Good evening, Inspector. As the countess says, your arrival is unexpected. I hope you have a good reason for bursting in on us in this discourteous fashion. I would remind you I'm a British officer and the countess is a member of the aristocracy.'

His glance went to the gun. 'And by the way, I'd be obliged if you'd stop waving that damned thing around.'

De Silva lowered the Webley's barrel but kept a close eye on Aubrey. He was determined not to fall into the trap of letting the major rattle him.

'I believe I have a very good reason for coming, Major Aubrey. I have questions for you and Miss Lane.'

If Laetitia Lane was shocked, she concealed it well. A clipped British accent replaced the Italian one.

'So, you've discovered my identity, Inspector. Did the count tell you about our little charade? How very ungallant of him. He might have had the decency to spare my blushes.'

De Silva wondered whether this was what she really believed. If so, it indicated that he was dealing with a simple case of jewellery theft. If, however, she had noticed her possessions had been searched, there might be more to it than that. For the moment, he decided to play along.

'Perhaps if you hadn't relieved him of a considerable fortune in jewels, ma'am, he might have been more inclined to do so.'

Laetitia Lane threw back her head, displaying her long, creamy neck to its best advantage. She let out a peal of musical laughter. The lady hadn't been an actress for nothing, thought de Silva.

'What nonsense. He gave me the jewels to wear while I was with him but they're still in his possession. If he claims otherwise, he's a liar.'

'And a cad,' added Aubrey. His face had darkened and the veins stood out on his neck.

'Nevertheless, I must search your luggage.'

Aubrey started forward. 'How dare you, sir.'

Laetitia Lane put a restraining hand on Aubrey's shoulder. 'James, let them search. We have nothing to hide.'

There was a menacing pause. Aubrey glowered; he clenched his fists then finally relaxed them and let his hands fall to his sides. 'If Letty has no objection, I suppose you may,' he muttered.

'But I assure you,' said Laetitia Lane calmly, 'you won't find as much as a single earring.'

De Silva felt perplexed. Either she was a very good actress or as innocent as she claimed to be. Well, there was nothing for it but to start the search. Yet what if the jewels weren't anywhere readily accessible? He could hardly demand to search Miss Lane's person.

'Nadar, go down and tell the owner I want a spare room made ready for Major Aubrey and Miss Lane.'

'I know our rights, Inspector,' said Aubrey. 'I insist we're present while you search.'

'We don't both need to be here, James. I'll stay.'

'No, I should be the one to handle this.'

She touched his cheek. 'Let's not argue about it. I'm sure I shall be perfectly safe in the inspector's hands.'

With a show of reluctance, Major Aubrey went to the room the owner offered. Satisfied the door was securely locked, de Silva returned to where he had left Nadar on guard and commenced his search.

Laetitia Lane lounged in a chair smoking a cigarette. She waved it in the direction of the door by the bed. 'Our cases are in there, Inspector, but they're all empty. Major Aubrey and I travel light. What we have with us is in those drawers and that cupboard. I doubt your search will take long.'

Noticing how Nadar didn't raise his eyes from his feet, de Silva decided to spare him the embarrassment of searching a lady's room in her presence and sent him to check the suitcases.

'It was clever of you to find us, Inspector,' remarked Laetitia Lane, as he opened drawers. She was right: there was very little to look through. He'd go through the motions but it was quite possible she was concealing the pouch with the jewellery under the robe; it was of a very generous cut. He'd have to enlist Jane's help, but all in good time. Laetitia Lane wasn't going anywhere now. He'd make sure of that.

'You flatter me, ma'am.'

'Oh, surely not.'

'I suppose all my acquaintances in Nuala believe I'm a thief and an impostor?' She tapped the ash off her cigarette. 'How shocked poor dear Florence Clutterbuck must have been.'

'I've no idea, ma'am. I wasn't present when she was informed the jewels were missing.'

'You're very diplomatic, Inspector.' She paused to inhale then let out a puff of smoke. 'Perhaps the count told you I was an actress? I was in a play in the West End once – a dreadful piece called *Murder at Middleton Grange*. It flopped and was taken off after a few nights. I played the part of a woman who murdered her unfaithful husband.'

'Most interesting.' He closed the cupboard and, going to the bed, picked up a pillow and prodded it.

'Not really, but I do recall one amusing detail. My character suspected her drawers would be searched for the murder weapon. She planned to throw it in the lake the next day but hid it in a drawer overnight. To make sure she knew if anyone tampered with the drawer, she placed a single hair across the join in the wood.'

Ah, so there was more to it than theft.

'I understand from my wife who is a great reader of detective novels that the strategy you describe is a much-overused plot device.'

She stubbed out her cigarette. 'I did say the play was dreadful.'

'May I?' He indicated the bedsheets.

'Please, strip it all off if you want. I expect you'll want your constable's help with the mattress. I do hope the British government agrees to compensate the owner here if you insist on slitting it open.'

'I hope that won't be necessary.'

'Good.'

She lit a fresh cigarette and he smelt Russian tobacco. 'Going back to the single hair, I suppose it works?'

'I imagine so, ma'am.'

'So, by that analogy, a very small thing might provide a clue in solving a mystery? Say if someone observant was to notice that one of their possessions wasn't quite as it had been the last time they looked at it?'

De Silva felt sure now. She was thinking of the crocodile-skin bag. She'd noticed that the stitching was too clumsy and guessed someone had tampered with it.

He glanced up and found she was giving him a ravishing smile. 'What do you think, Inspector? I'd value your professional opinion.'

To his annoyance, he found he was lost for words.

Her smile widened.

CHAPTER 18

The Morris's headlights lit up the sweep of drive in front of the bungalow as he returned home to Sunnybank. The door opened and Jane hurried out.

'Shanti! I thought I heard the car. Where have you been all this time? Archie Clutterbuck has been trying to get hold of you.'

'Searching for Laetitia Lane, of course. As he wanted me to.'

'Did you find her?'

'Yes, and Major Aubrey was with her.'

'Gracious, so I was right, there is something between them.'

'That appears to be the case. I found them together in a guest house in town, but so far I've had no luck finding the jewellery. She must have hidden it very cleverly. I'll need to ask you to search her if she doesn't give it up.'

'Oh, that won't be necessary now.'

'What do you mean?'

'We know where it is.'

De Silva groaned. He seemed fated to waste time over this woman. 'Where?' he asked testily.

'In the guest bungalow after all. You remember I told you how much Florence disliked the count? She insisted on organising a search in case there was some mistake. The count wasn't pleased at all but not much stands in

Florence's way when she's made up her mind about something. Anyway, I was asked to help and even Lady Caroline became involved. I don't believe she has much time for the count either.'

She chuckled. 'Angel was in attendance too. Whenever I see Florence, he's never far behind. We found nothing at first and the count was blustering about how offended he was and he'd a good mind to complain to the governor. Then Angel started yapping. We couldn't see where he was until I spotted his bottom sticking out from under an ottoman in the bedroom. Florence was in a terrible state. She thought he was stuck and called for some servants to lift the ottoman.'

'What was it?'

'There was a hump in the rug. Angel was pawing and sniffing at it, wagging his tail in great excitement. I picked him up and gave him to Florence then the servants rolled back the rug. Underneath it was a pouch with the jewellery neatly stored inside. I thought the count would explode he went so red, but there wasn't much he could say. Everything he claimed had been stolen was there. He tried to make up some story but it was obvious to everyone that he'd invented the whole thing because he was furious with Miss Lane for running off. Florence was delighted and even Archie made a bit of a fuss of Angel. Angel seemed very pleased with that. Perhaps they'll even be good friends one day. But it still leaves the letter and those passports. Was there no sign of them?'

'Not a trace. Either she had them under her clothes or she'd got rid of them.'

'What will you do now?'

'Do? I think I'll have a whisky and soda. Archie Clutterbuck made it abundantly clear that when the matter of the jewellery was settled, my services would no longer be required.'

Jane looked at him sympathetically. 'It's not like you to give up, Shanti.'

'Oh, I don't see it as giving up; I've done my bit. It's a British problem now.'

'It is rather fun being proved right about Laetitia Lane and Major Aubrey, don't you think?'

'It was a lucky guess.'

'I prefer to call it an educated one.'

'Alright, it was very clever of you. Obviously, I'd do far better to stay here and read detective novels than chase about the countryside.'

She tucked her arm in his. 'You're cross.'

'Yes, I suppose I am. This whole thing is a mess and I've wasted too much time on the count and his lies.'

She reached up and kissed his cheek. 'My poor dear. Never mind. The count won't be here much longer, and neither, I suspect, will Laetitia Lane or Major Aubrey.'

'But there will still be the problem of Helen Wynne-Talbot.'

Jane sighed. 'I fear so.'

'I should go and see Archie Clutterbuck,' he said with a grimace.

'You do that, then we'll have dinner.'

* * *

Fortified by a whisky, he set off a quarter of an hour later. At the Residence, the house lights cast a buttery glow on the gravel and the façade looked a particularly pristine white against the dark sky. He parked the car and went to the door. A servant came swiftly to answer the bell. The sight of de Silva in uniform clearly surprised him.

'Sahib is not here,' he said, when de Silva asked for Clutterbuck.

'Will he be out all evening?'

'Yes. He and the memsahib attend a dinner at the British club.'

It would cause a stir if he tried to flush the assistant government agent out of a dinner at the club. He pictured the speculation at the card tables and in the smoking room. Clutterbuck wouldn't thank him for it. No, this would have to wait until tomorrow and damn the consequences. He hoped he was making the right decision and his caution wouldn't arouse Clutterbuck's ire once again. He nodded to the servant. 'Please tell him Inspector de Silva called and will telephone in the morning.'

The man bowed. 'Yes, sahib.'

De Silva hesitated. 'On second thoughts, I'll leave a message for him. I'd better come in. Find me a pen and paper.'

The servant showed him through to a small room to one side of the entrance hall and left to fetch the writing materials. When he returned, de Silva composed a brief message explaining he was aware that the jewellery had been found but he had detained Aubrey and Miss Lane regardless as he presumed Clutterbuck would still want to question them, both in relation to Helen Wynne-Talbot's death and to their activities in Nuala.

He read the note over, signed it and put it in the envelope the servant had provided. 'See to it that your master gets this on his return.'

Passing an uneasy night, he pictured Major Aubrey and Laetitia Lane penned up at the guest house. He hoped he had made the right decision. His prisoners were bound to want someone on whom to vent their displeasure and, unless Clutterbuck took his part, he would be right in the line of fire.

Everything depended on how Clutterbuck approached the situation. He might be very pleased Aubrey and Miss

Lane were still in British hands, alternatively he might want to allay Miss Lane's suspicions by setting her free. If that's the case, thought de Silva, he'll probably make a show of censuring me, but I must endure that.

He rolled over and curled up like a caterpillar but sleep still eluded him. Instead, the image of Florence's beloved Angel cavorted through his mind, dragging in its teeth a seemingly endless string of diamonds that sparkled as brightly as the little dog's beady eyes. Floating behind, Helen Wynne-Talbot's pale, seraphic face accused him with its sorrowful expression.

Eventually, unable to endure any more, he slipped out of bed, moving stealthily so as not to wake Jane. In the bathroom, he took his robe from the hook by the door and put it on then pushed his feet into his slippers. Except for the tick of the clock in the hall, the bungalow was silent. A shaft of moonlight fell like an arrow on the drawing room floor, pointing the way to the verandah. He turned the key in the lock and went outside. In April, the air rarely cooled as much at night as it did earlier in the year and he wasn't cold.

Moonlight leached the colour from the trees and flowers so that the garden looked like a faded print. Night-time, however, intensified its scents. Drinking them in, he felt at peace. He was so lucky to have this haven from the squabbles and demands of the human race. He had done his best to do the right thing and he would weather any storms that resulted. If Archie Clutterbuck chose not to support him after all, so be it.

Idly, he wondered whether Laetitia Lane really was a traitor to her country. Jane sometimes spoke of the Great War and the terrible loss of life incurred. The loser, Germany, had sunk into an economic depression, but in the last few years, Adolf Hitler's National Socialists had come to power, promising to restore Germany's greatness. Many people mistrusted Hitler, but there were some, and they included members of the British aristocracy, who admired the man. Was Laetitia Lane one of them?

He shivered and reminded himself that, although he had to serve the British in Ceylon, their problems in Europe were, fortunately, outside his remit. After a last turn round the garden, he went indoors and returned to bed.

CHAPTER 19

His head muzzy from his restless night, de Silva drank two cups of strong tea but hardly touched his breakfast. Jane looked at him with dismay. 'Try not to worry, dear. I'm sure it will all work out for the best.'

'I expect you're right,' he said, trying to infuse his voice with more confidence than he felt. He put down his crumpled napkin and got up from the table. 'I'd better get off to the station and find out if there's a message. Not much point seeing Aubrey and Miss Lane until I know how the land lies.'

The station door was still locked for he had left Nadar on guard at the guest house in case Aubrey or Miss Lane took it into their heads to persuade the owner to let them out. So, one person at least had benefited from the situation, he thought wryly. Last night had probably been the quietest Nadar had enjoyed in a long time.

He had just made himself some tea and taken it to his office when Nadar arrived. De Silva frowned. 'What are you doing here, Constable? Didn't I tell you to watch the prisoners?'

'I'm sorry, sir. Mr Clutterbuck came and sent me away. He told me to tell you that you are not needed at the guest house and he will speak with you later.'

De Silva's spirits sank. This didn't bode well.

The day was well advanced when Clutterbuck telephoned.

Cautiously, de Silva wished him good afternoon.

'It's a tolerable one now, I suppose,' came the gruff reply. 'In spite of the fact that I've spent most of the day smoothing ruffled feathers when I could have been fishing. Didn't I tell you to back off from Major Aubrey? Instead I find that you've incarcerated him in some flea-bitten guest house!'

De Silva bit his tongue. The guest house hadn't been of his choosing and, in any case, it had seemed to him to be perfectly clean and respectable.

'Miss Lane too, even though you were aware she was cleared of theft.'

'Sir, I explained in my note to you, I didn't want to release them without your authority.'

'Why didn't you call me out of the club last night?'

'I was concerned it would give rise to unwelcome curiosity.'

Clutterbuck grunted. 'I suppose you're not to blame. I didn't know the truth myself until Colombo filled me in. It seems our Major Aubrey is a hero with a distinguished record of service on the North-West frontier. After several successful missions, he was captured and handled pretty roughly by the Afghans. I understand he was lucky to escape with his life.'

De Silva remembered the scars he'd noticed on Aubrey's chest and everything became clear. For as long as he could remember, the British had been wrangling with Russia over Afghanistan, the gateway to India. The author they were so fond of, Rudyard Kipling, had called it the Great Game. How was he supposed to know Aubrey had been involved in it?

'Laetitia Lane turns out to be one of ours too. She was tasked with finding out more about the count and his German connections and Aubrey was helping her. It was all going well until she suspected someone had searched her room. That must have been you, of course, but she had no way of knowing it at the time. It was only when you interviewed her later that she suspected the truth. Initially, she was afraid she'd been unmasked by some unfriendly agent, so between her and Aubrey, they'd decided it was time to get out.'

Clutterbuck's voice tailed off and there was a considerable pause before he spoke again.

'De Silva?'

'Yes, sir?'

The rumble of a throat being cleared came down the line. 'I've decided we'll say no more about it. By now they will have left Nuala and hopefully the whole sorry mess is behind us.'

De Silva felt a mixture of relief and frustration.

'Getting back to the Wynne-Talbot woman. Have you found her body yet?'

'No, sir.'

'Try to hurry it up, de Silva. It would be good to show William Petrie that we can get something right up here.'

There was a click at the end of the line. De Silva replaced the receiver and the teacup rattled in its saucer. He picked up a pencil and flexed it; the lead snapped.

He spent the remainder of the afternoon dealing irritably with minor matters until Nadar put his head round the door.

'Sergeant Prasanna's back, sir.'

'What news?'

'He's found the lady's body, sir.'

'Send him in.'

'He has two people with him, sir.'

'Oh? They'd better come in too.'

Prasanna was first into the room. His uniform shorts and shirt were somewhat grimy and dust dulled the shine on his boots. He acknowledged de Silva's glance at them with an apologetic expression. 'I'm sorry, sir, I came straight here. I thought you'd want to know as soon as possible.'

'You were right; the assistant government agent has been pressing me. Where did you find the body?'

'In one of the places where we looked first, sir. I had almost given up when one of the villagers saw her. I think her fall must have been broken by trees growing out of the rock. There was very little injury.' He shook his head sadly. 'When we found her, if I had not known otherwise, I would have thought she was asleep.'

De Silva felt relieved. If the husband wanted to be the one who formally identified her, it might be less of an ordeal for him if the body wasn't too badly damaged.

'Where is she now?'

'She has been taken to the hospital, sir. Doctor Hebden sent this for you.'

Prasanna handed over a piece of paper and de Silva ran his eye down the doctor's scrawled acknowledgement and recommendation that a funeral be arranged as soon as possible.

'I'll notify the assistant government agent and he can deal with the family. Well done, Prasanna. I'm sure it wasn't an easy or a pleasant job.'

'No, sir. Thank you, sir.'

De Silva glanced at the doorway where a young man and a girl in a yellow sari waited quietly. 'Who's this you've brought with you?'

Prasanna led the girl forward. De Silva racked his brains; he was sure he recognised her. Ah yes, the yellow sari. On the day he and Jane had gone dancing, he'd noticed this girl and her beautiful eyes as he drove through the bazaar.

'Sir, this is my friend Kuveni,' said Prasanna tentatively. 'And this is Vijay, her brother.'

CHAPTER 20

'Bring up a chair for the lady.' De Silva smiled at the girl and she gave him a shy smile in return.

Prasanna fetched a chair and held it out for her solicitously.

'Shall we speak in Tamil or Sinhalese?' de Silva asked when she had sat down. Prasanna and Vijay remained standing on either side of her.

'Sinhalese, sir,' said Prasanna.

'So, your friends are Sinhalese?'

'No, we are Vedda,' the girl said in a soft voice.

Ah, that wouldn't make life any easier for them, thought de Silva. The Veddas were an ancient race, but often looked down on by the other occupants of Ceylon who considered them a backward people. Historically, they had lived by hunting and were nomads, but now some of them had settled and grew crops on small patches of jungle that they cleared with axes and fire. They weren't welcome in many villages and were rarely seen in the towns. He wasn't surprised to hear that the headman was making trouble for Kuveni and her family.

'What do you want to see me about?' he asked, looking at the girl.

'It is about their troubles with the headman of their village, as I told you, sir,' Prasanna intervened.

De Silva held up his hand. 'Let her speak for herself.'

There was an expression of quiet determination on Kuveni's face as she began.

'My family used to live in a village in the jungle. It is a day's walk from Nuala. We did not have very much, but my brother and my father cleared a piece of land each year so that we could grow millet or maize and some vegetables. I helped with the digging and planting and occasionally we had a little meat from hunting.'

Neither the brother nor the sister appeared to have suffered from their simple diet. Both looked healthier than many of the poor Tamils and Sinhalese de Silva saw in town. The girl wasn't only blessed with a pretty face, she had thick, glossy hair and clear skin. The brother, Vijay, looked strong and supple. His black hair stood out like a bush around his narrow, finely-featured face.

'From the earliest I remember, the headman made life difficult for my father. When it was time for getting the government permits, we were always the last in line. He also demanded a larger share of what we grew than he made the rest of the village give.'

De Silva frowned. He knew it was common practice for village headmen to take a proportion of their villagers' produce as payment for carrying out their duties. These included applying to the British for the permits without which it was illegal to clear and cultivate land, but the amount taken was supposed to be reasonable and not harder on one family than another.

'Eventually, my father went to him and asked why he was treating us like this. We had never made any trouble for him.'

'What was the headman's answer?'

'He said my father was making his complaints up. It was foolish of him because we are Veddas and the villagers did not want us there anyway. It was only because of his goodness to us that we were not driven out.'

She grimaced. 'His goodness to us! There is no goodness in that man.'

Her brother had been listening intently but de Silva wasn't sure how well he understood the conversation. The girl's command of Sinhalese was impressive.

'How did you learn to speak the language?' he asked her.

'From the women in the village. They love to talk when they are together making food or collecting water. I listened.'

'I interrupted you. Go on.'

'Then the headman's wife died.' She looked down. 'He said that I pleased him. If I would go and live with him, he would see to it that the other villagers treated us well. By which he meant he would treat us well.'

'But you didn't accept him?'

The girl shook her head and he saw tears on her cheeks. 'I asked my father what I must do but he wouldn't speak about it. I decided to say no, and then the headman was very angry. He made life even harder for us and I was afraid I would have to agree after all, but while I was still unsure, he accused my father of stealing from him and had us chased from the village.'

'Where is your father now?'

'Here in Nuala, but he would not come with us to see you. He does nothing but sit all day. Everything is hard for him and he says he cannot breathe with buildings and people everywhere. At night he has bad dreams. We are very worried about him.'

'Kuveni is afraid he will harm himself,' said Prasanna.

'Why do you think that?' asked de Silva gently.

'His spirit has been broken by all the troubles. What the headman said was a lie, but some people, the ones who do not like us because we are Veddas, were ready to believe it. My father had already stopped laughing and telling us the old stories and songs. Now he says we would be better off without him.'

She fell silent. With a sigh, de Silva turned to her brother. 'Do you understand what your sister's told me?'

The young man nodded.

'And is it the truth?'

Another nod.

He addressed Kuveni once more. 'How are you making money to live?'

'One of the sari makers in the bazaar gives me work. It's harder for Vijay because, although he understands some Sinhalese and Tamil, he does not speak any language but our own. He gets work delivering vegetables.'

'You must tell the inspector about Vijay's other work, Kuveni,' prompted Prasanna. 'It is important he knows what Vijay saw.'

A wary expression came over Kuveni's face. She twisted a fold of her sari. 'He has friends who help him sometimes. They are shikaris for the British when they do their hunting. Vijay was always the best at tracking. If he goes with them, they give him some of the money they are paid but he has to be careful not to be noticed.'

De Silva put down his pen and scratched his head. He shouldn't condone what the young man was doing. The Europeans and Americans who came to Ceylon for the hunting were invariably well off and usually generous with their tips, provided that their trackers did a good job and found them plenty of game to massacre. Accordingly, tracking jobs were highly sought after and jealously guarded. Under the British system for regulating hunting, they were supposed to be parcelled out by village headmen. No wonder Vijay didn't want to be noticed.

'Why are you telling me this?'

'Because Vijay was at World's End on the night when the English lady died. He saw her fall but then he ran away because he should not have been there.'

De Silva felt a surge of interest; he scrutinised Kuveni.

'Please ask your brother to say exactly what he saw. It's important he understands the question and doesn't miss out anything he remembers.'

Kuveni spoke rapidly to Vijay who answered at some length.

'He says he saw the British lady come out of her tent. She stood for a few moments but she seemed to be in a dream as if she was not awake. She walked very slowly towards the precipice. Some of the ground she walked on was sharp with stones. Creeping plants grow there that will give you pain if you are not used to going barefoot. But the lady took no notice and kept on walking. A man came out of one of the other tents. Vijay saw it was the British officer. By the time he noticed the British lady, she was standing at the edge. She turned once. Vijay does not know if she saw he was there. Then she was gone.'

'Please thank your brother. His information is very helpful. I promise you his name won't go outside this room.'

Kuveni looked relieved.

De Silva leant back in his chair with a frown. This new evidence was very interesting. From the scene the young man described, it was possible that Mrs Wynne-Talbot had been sleepwalking. Her slow pace and obliviousness to pain could be indications that she was in a trance. But then, as he and Clutterbuck had discussed just after her death, sleepwalkers were known to retain a sense of self-preservation, so why would that be absent in this case? Might there be drugs involved? Yet none had been found in her tent.

He turned the possibilities over in his mind then finally settled on suicide. With what Helen Wynne-Talbot's husband had told them about his wife's state of mind, it seemed the most likely cause of death. But why did he still feel that something wasn't quite right? Was there unfinished business? A loose end left untied?

He put the thought out of his mind. He was seeing conspiracies where there were none. Fortunately, as Clutterbuck needed no further convincing of Mrs Wynne-Talbot's suicide, keeping Vijay's secret safe was easier. Normally he would agree that regulations should be upheld, but in this case, they could go hang. All that remained was to do what he could to help this brother and sister.

'I'll speak again with the assistant government agent,' he said.

A look of anxiety crossed Kuveni's face.

'As I said, there will be no need to explain to him that your brother was at World's End.'

'Thank you, sir.'

'You may go now. I assume my sergeant knows where to find you?'

She nodded.

'Then I'll send him to you when there's news. Prasanna, come back here when you've shown your friends out.'

'I didn't want to dash their hopes,' he said when Prasanna returned. 'But I'm afraid I'm not very optimistic.'

His sergeant looked downcast. 'But you will try, sir?'

'Of course, I've said I will.'

Prasanna's eyes swivelled to the window and the view of Kuveni and Vijay walking away from the station. The girl's slim figure and pretty face turned many heads as she went by. It was easy to see why Prasanna was keen to impress her with his usefulness, but he must be aware that he was heading into deep waters. With his mother's ideas about suitable girls, she was bound to disapprove strongly. He wanted to give the lad some advice, tell him Kuveni wasn't the only girl in the world. But of course there was no point. Anyone could see that the boy was head over heels in love. All the time she had been speaking, his eyes had never left her face. As far as he was concerned, no one else mattered.

He cleared his throat. 'I expect your mother will be pleased to have you home. After your good work on the

Wynne-Talbot case, I'll see to it you're rewarded with a bonus.'

Prasanna thanked him and departed, but the prospect of a bonus didn't seem to have cheered him much.

CHAPTER 21

At home, he and Jane sat on the verandah drinking tea as he brought her up to date with the news about Helen Wynne-Talbot, Laetitia Lane and James Aubrey.

'Gracious, it all sounds very dramatic about Miss Lane and Major Aubrey,' she said when he had finished. 'Just like the plot of a film. Do you know where they'll go now?'

'They've already left Nuala, but for where, I have no idea.'

'Perhaps they'll be retired to some sleepy village in the English countryside as they would be in a novel. Or maybe the South of France to enjoy their reward from a grateful government.'

De Silva grinned. 'I imagine Laetitia Lane would choose the second option every time.'

'No doubt.' She sighed. 'So we can all settle down happily again, except, of course, for poor Ralph Wynne-Talbot. Florence told me there's been news from England. His grandfather has died. It's so sad they will never meet. Florence says Lady Caroline intends to travel back to England with him after the funeral. I expect he'll be glad of her support. He'll have to take his seat in the House of Lords as well as taking charge of the Axford estate.'

'Hmm, yes. I suppose he will have a lot to think about.'

'Sergeant Prasanna must be relieved to be back in Nuala. I hope you gave him plenty of praise.'

'I did, but I can't say he's very happy.'

'What do you mean?'

'Poor lad,' she said when he reached the end of the story. 'Even if he does find that this girl cares for him, he'll have to get round his mother. From what I've seen of her, that won't be easy.'

'No, it won't. At least the Prasannas are Buddhists, so, strictly speaking, there ought not to be a problem of caste as there would be if they were Hindu. But that's not to say there'll be no prejudice, especially as the girl is from the Vedda people.'

They lapsed into silence. 'I do hope something can be done,' remarked Jane after a while. 'It must be hard for them, living among strangers.'

'No doubt, although I believe the girl will adapt given time. If she's already managing skilled work, she might do well in the end.'

'You liked her, didn't you?'

'I suppose I did. She hasn't had any advantages in life but she seems intelligent and polite. The sort of person one would like to help.'

'Perhaps she might even be better off staying in Nuala.'

'Who knows? Certainly Prasanna would be delighted.'

'Do you think Archie Clutterbuck will help them?'

He frowned. At the moment he was in no position to press Archie Clutterbuck to do anything, but hopefully time would change that. Anyway, he didn't want to say too much and make Jane worry.

'He's a decent man. I expect he'll agree to look into it eventually. When all the excitement's over, I'll bring the subject up again and see how he reacts.'

'Good.'

She shivered.

'What's wrong?'

'I was just thinking about poor Helen Wynne-Talbot. She must have been very unhappy to take her own life. I can't imagine what she was thinking as she walked towards that precipice.'

'If Vijay is right, there might have been nothing going through her mind.'

'You mean she was sleepwalking, or had worked herself up into some kind of trance?'

'There have been many instances of that at religious festivals here and in India. People's minds depart from their bodies and they harm themselves without feeling pain.'

'But Helen Wynne-Talbot was British.'

'I agree it would not be a British way of behaving, so, in answer to your question, I think it's extremely unlikely. It was early morning and only just getting light. Vijay may not have seen Mrs Wynne-Talbot's face as clearly as he thinks he did. People from the villages are very superstitious, Vedda people more than most. Vijay probably finds it impossible to credit that anyone would harm themselves unless a devil had entered their body.'

Jane sighed. 'I suppose we shouldn't be too quick to mock. After all, there's a great deal we Europeans don't understand about mental illness.'

He got to his feet; suddenly he was weary of talking about the case. It had been a waste of time and worse still, for the moment, it had probably lost him Archie Clutterbuck's goodwill.

'Do I have time for a walk around the garden before dinner?'

'Plenty of time. I've been teaching Cook to prepare some new dishes and I thought we'd have one of them tonight: chicken fricassée. I told him to take his time and it won't be ready for at least an hour.'

She picked up her book. 'Oh, and dear,' she added, 'if you're planning to be out for long, would you change your shoes? It's cooling down and there'll soon be dew on the grass.'

He went to the bedroom to change his shoes then returned to the drawing room. Surreptitiously, he opened the silver cigarette box that Jane liked to keep for visitors. He took out a cigarette then went to the garden by the side door. Once he was outside, he lit the cigarette and inhaled, drawing the pungent smoke deep into his lungs. He couldn't remember when he'd last smoked – Jane preferred him not to – but just now, he needed the calming effect of tobacco.

That expectant hush that foreshadows night had descended on the garden. As he wandered between the flowerbeds, daylight faded. He stopped to smell a chrysanthemum that had opened fully since that morning: a sunburst of shell-pink petals, each one tightly furled like the paper spills the servants used to light the fires in winter. After roses, chrysanthemums were his favourites. He remembered how his mother used to boil up the flowers to make a fragrant tea. She'd sworn by it as a cure for headaches and sore throats. When he was a teenager and hard to rouse in the mornings, she'd always brought him a steaming cup to wake him up ready for school.

He wondered what she would have thought of his marrying an Englishwoman. She'd been both kind and generous, but he suspected that, like Sergeant Prasanna's mother, she would have preferred him to settle down with a nice Sinhalese girl. His father, a policeman too, might have been more accepting. His work would have brought him into contact with the British whereas his mother spent her time in the house or with her Sinhalese friends.

The regret he always felt when he thought of his father came over him. He wished he'd known him better; he'd been a schoolboy when he died. He would have liked to talk to him about how he had dealt with his British masters. Had there been times when he'd found it hard to steer the right course?

A flock of egrets flew over, flapping lazily towards the

rosy glow in the west. He heard the distant screech of a peacock and another answering it.

One by one, the lights were going on in the town below. He walked to the end of the garden and stood by the privet hedge watching them. The words of a hymn they had sung at church the last time he went with Jane slipped into his head:

When upon life's billows you are tempest tossed,
When you are discouraged, thinking all is lost,
Count your blessings, name them one by one,
Count your blessings, see what God has done!

Then something he couldn't quite remember about conflicts great or small. He sighed. Did he invite problems? He had never thought so but certainly his assumption that life in Nuala would be peaceful and uncomplicated hadn't proved to be correct. Perhaps he must accept that people made life complicated wherever you were.

He looked back at the bungalow. The lamps on the verandah glowed and Jane still sat there, calmly reading her book. He hoped he was going to enjoy this chicken fricassée. The last English recipe Cook had served for dinner – Lancashire hotpot – had been moderately enlivened by the presence of plenty of onions but he still preferred a good fiery curry. Still, Jane had accustomed herself to his country's food so he ought to make the effort in return.

A figure appeared in the doorway to the verandah. Jane closed her book and waved. Dinner must be ready; he should go inside and wash his hands. As he crossed the lawn, it suddenly dawned on him why he had felt that something remained unfinished, even after young Vijay confirmed that Helen Wynne-Talbot had jumped.

It was the anonymous caller to the station who had spoken to Nadar. He hadn't telephoned back. Perhaps he was just a crank; one of those tiresome people who needed to bolster their sense of importance by pretending to know something about a case that no one else did, but, in some obscure way, the silence bothered him.

The chicken fricassée turned out to be pleasant, with a silky sauce and plenty of vegetables and chopped herbs. To de Silva's mind, however, some chillies would have vastly improved the mild, grassy flavours. When dinner was over, he and Jane retired to the drawing room to read. After a surfeit of the muscular works of Sir Walter Scott, he wanted a change and Jane had suggested he try Jane Austen. He was reading *Pride and Prejudice* which he was enjoying far more than he had expected. He understood from Jane that Sir Walter had been a great admirer of Miss Austen's works, as she had been of his, in spite of the fact that their novels could not be more different.

He found the place where he had stopped the previous evening and settled into a new chapter. When it came to the end, he let the book fall in his lap and rested his eyes for a few moments. They felt rather scratchy this evening, perhaps the lingering effects of that dusty walk up to Horton Plains, even though it seemed like a lifetime ago.

He wondered what Miss Austen had been like: an acerbic lady perhaps. Her observation of the workings of the human heart was perceptive and her eye for folly sharp. Would he have enjoyed meeting her? It might have been an unnerving experience. Perhaps he would have been as incapable of holding an interesting and rational conversation with her as dull Mr Collins or giddy Lydia.

Jane looked up from her Agatha Christie. 'How are you getting on?'

'Very well. It's an excellent novel. As you said, a pleasant change from Sir Walter.'

'Where have you got to?'

'Darcy's formidable aunt has just arrived at Longbourn to find out whether Elizabeth Bennet is hoping to marry him.' He grinned. 'I notice that in literature it's frequently aunts who are cast as the villains – P G Wodehouse is another example – whereas uncles are mostly amiable.'

Jane sniffed. 'I hope you're not implying anything.'

'Of course not.'

'Just as well.'

She closed her book and stifled a yawn. 'I'll save the rest for tomorrow.' She rested her chin on her hand pensively.

'Sixpence for them?'

'A penny, dear, it's all they're worth anyway. I was just thinking about Sergeant Prasanna again. It seems very harsh that he might have to give up this girl to please his mother.'

He shrugged. 'Yes, but who knows? The girl may not even be keen on him in the first place.'

'Oh, surely she will be. Your sergeant's a good-looking young man and you always say he has a bright future if he stays in the force.'

'I believe he does, but that doesn't mean the girl will feel the same way about him as he does about her.'

'I suppose you're right.'

He returned to his book but when he looked up again, Jane was still sitting in her chair, with the same thoughtful expression on her face.

'What is it now? I hope you're not turning into a Mrs Bennet, fretting about marrying her daughters off. There's no point worrying about Prasanna and his love life. He's old enough to stand up to his mother if this girl's the one he really wants.'

'Actually, I wasn't thinking about him any longer, I was thinking about Ralph Wynne-Talbot.'

'What about him?'

'I was wondering if he will marry again.'

'I should think it's rather more a question of when.'

'Shanti!'

'Oh, I don't mean that unkindly, but won't he need a

wife to help with this great house he will inherit? Who will manage it for him?'

Jane raised an eyebrow. 'I'd like to think a wife is something more than a housekeeper.'

He put his book on the table beside his chair, reached out and pulled her onto his lap. 'I can't answer for the British aristocracy, but mine certainly is.'

She stroked his hair. 'I'm very glad to hear it. And I expect you're right about Ralph Wynne-Talbot. It will be a lonely life if he doesn't find someone to share it with, and I'm sure every mother of unmarried daughters in England will be eager to help him do so.'

CHAPTER 22

It rained steadily in the night. In the morning, the garden smelt of damp earth and grass, and birds darted between shimmering trees. As the Morris purred along the road into town, the beauty of the day dispelled de Silva's gloom.

Nadar was already at the station but there was no sign of Prasanna. 'He has gone to the bazaar, sir,' Nadar said uncomfortably when de Silva asked where his colleague was.

'Oh? Is there some trouble there?'

'I'm not sure, sir. Maybe monkeys are stealing from the stalls again,' Nadar added lamely.

De Silva's lips twitched. He had a pretty good idea what had drawn Prasanna to the bazaar. 'Well, let's hope those criminal masterminds aren't too difficult to foil, eh Nadar?'

'No, sir. I mean yes, sir.' A guilty look came over his round, earnest face. 'Forgive me, sir, I do not believe that is really why he's gone.'

'Nor do I; no doubt he wants to see this young lady of his again.'

Nadar's guilty look changed to one of concern. 'I hope it will not mean trouble for him, sir. His mother has very strong opinions. It was easy for my wife and me, our families approved of the match. In fact, they were all most anxious for it.'

'That was very fortunate for you.'

'Yes, sir, I am a very lucky man.'

De Silva clapped him on the back. 'Good. Now don't you worry about Sergeant Prasanna, he must fight his own battles.' He opened the door to his office. 'I expect to be in all morning. Bring my tea, will you?'

'Yes, sir.'

De Silva went to his desk and sat down. After Prasanna had spent the last few days tramping about the jungle on his grisly errand, he probably deserved a bit of latitude. He'd turn a blind eye for a day or two, but then in fairness to Nadar, Prasanna would have to pull his weight again.

He spent a few minutes going through his post until there was a knock at the door and Nadar arrived with the tea. When he'd gone, de Silva opened the bulky envelope at the bottom of the pile. It was the catalogue he'd ordered from Colombo. He leafed through the pages, admiring the fine range of gramophones the company offered. Some came in tall cabinets, others were designed to sit on table tops or even be portable. The more ornate ones were made of waxed oak adorned with gilt fittings. Delicate patterns of leaves and flowers had been incised on their horns.

His Majesty's Voice: the company symbolised the best of British manufacturing. Even the famous Sir Edward Elgar lauded their products as the only way to listen to music for those not fortunate enough to have the opportunity of going to the best concert halls to enjoy it.

He studied the technical details – apparently, the machines had been furnished with a new type of sound box that gave equal balance to treble and bass and virtually eliminated the hisses and crackles he'd noticed on the few gramophones he had heard played. He also considered the look of the machines and finally came to his decision, choosing one with a pretty, octagonal-shaped case that was a good size for the place he had in mind. He mustn't leave it too long to send in his order. The gramophone would take time to arrive and he wanted to surprise Jane with it on their anniversary. Knowing how much she loved music, he was confident she'd be pleased. He leant back in his chair, picturing warm evenings on the verandah listening to the pieces they both loved, from dance music to opera, or even jazz.

There was another knock at the door and Nadar put his head round. 'There's someone to see you, sir. Shall I show him in?'

De Silva marked the page then closed the catalogue. He had an uneasy feeling. 'Who is it?'

Nadar lowered his voice. 'I think it may be the man who telephoned and wouldn't give his name, sir. He has the same voice.'

De Silva sighed. If the fellow had come in person, he'd better not turn him away without a hearing. 'Show him in, but warn him I'm busy and I can't spare him long. Better still, if he's not gone in ten minutes, knock on the door and say you wanted to remind me about an important engagement.'

The dark-haired man who entered the room looked British, probably about forty. His appearance was undistinguished, neither fat nor thin, in fact the most noticeable thing about him was that he walked with a pronounced limp.

De Silva rose from his chair. 'Good morning, sir. Please take a seat.'

'Thank you.' He noticed how the man winced as he dropped into the chair.

'Now, how may I help you?'

'I understand you're the officer who's been dealing with the investigation into the death of Helen Wynne-Talbot.'

Inwardly, de Silva groaned. This scenario was tediously familiar; he was about to hear some crackpot theory after all.

The man gave a wry smile. 'Your expression betrays you,

Inspector. No, I'm not mad and I haven't come to waste your time. On the contrary, I think you will find what I have to tell you very interesting.'

He cleared his throat. 'My name is Matthew Claybourne. I knew both Ralph and Helen Wynne-Talbot well. We spent several years together in Australia. Among other things, Ralph Wynne-Talbot and I were both engineers for a company involved in the construction of the Sydney Harbour Bridge.'

De Silva raised his hand. He would need a lot of convincing before he agreed to discuss the pros and cons of the Wynne-Talbot case with this man, even though he seemed more lucid than expected. For the moment, it was best to be as off-putting as possible. 'Before you go any further, Mr Claybourne, I ought to make it clear that the case is closed on Helen Wynne-Talbot's tragic death. The verdict, and we have reliable witnesses to substantiate it, was suicide. If it's your wish to pay your respects, the funeral will be held at St George's church here in Nuala in a few days. I'm sure you understand this is a very difficult time for Mr Wynne-Talbot. If you were a friend of his, may I suggest that you leave seeing him and offering your condolences until then?'

Claybourne smiled calmly. 'Oh, I assure you, Inspector de Silva, I have no intention of contacting Ralph Wynne-Talbot. In fact, it would be impossible for me to do so.'

'Why do you say that?' asked de Silva with a frown.

'For a very good reason, Inspector. Ralph Wynne-Talbot is dead.'

CHAPTER 23

It took de Silva a few seconds to recover his composure. He hoped he hadn't given Matthew Claybourne the satisfaction of thinking he had astonished him. In his experience, this kind of man lived for the excitement of feeling he was important. It had been a problem that the Colombo police had often had to address: how to sift the genuine informants from the charlatans.

'That's very interesting, Mr Claybourne, but do you have any proof?'

'I see you're not impressed, Inspector, and I can't say I blame you. Johnny Randall – he's the man who's masquerading as Ralph – is a clever fellow. Ever since I met him, I've been aware of his uncanny knack for pinpointing people's weaknesses. It didn't take him long to see that Ralph was vulnerable. He won his confidence early on in their acquaintance and learnt a lot about him. Certainly enough to do a convincing job of pretending to be him. And of course his task has been made much easier in Ceylon since Ralph's aunt and uncle never met him. Add to that Johnny's calculating charm, and the way he changes like a chameleon to win over whomever he's with, and the job is done.'

De Silva had to admit, Claybourne's assessment of the man he claimed was an impostor wasn't a million miles from his own. He remembered thinking on their first encounter at the Residence dinner that Helen Wynne-Talbot's husband's charm was too slick to be genuine. Afterwards, he'd wondered if he was just jealous that the man seemed so much more at ease in grand surroundings than he did himself, yet... He was careful not to show it but, in spite of his initial scepticism, his interest was aroused. He waited for Claybourne to continue but the man only stared blankly at an old ink stain on the desktop, as if he'd forgotten de Silva was there.

'It was convenient for him that he and Ralph looked very alike,' he said at last. 'If the Petries or any members of the Axford family had seen photographs of Ralph as a boy, it would be perfectly plausible that he grew up to look like Johnny. Their hair colour was different – Ralph was fair – but children's hair often darkens as they grow older. Anyway, given the family rift, Johnny probably thought it was a safe bet there were no photographs.'

He looked up and studied de Silva intently, as if trying to ascertain whether his story was being taken seriously. 'I'd better start at the beginning. I first met Helen and Ralph in Sydney. As I said, Ralph and I were both working on the Sydney Harbour Bridge project.'

De Silva nodded.

'I liked Ralph instantly and although Helen could be moody I spent a lot of time with them. The fact that Ralph and I were in the same line of work was a bond. He was never one to boast, in fact if anything people thought him a little too reserved, but he had a passion for what he did that struck a chord with me. We talked about moving on to Canberra when the bridge opened and the job ended. You may or may not know that about twenty years ago, in order to solve the rivalry between the cities of Sydney and Melbourne, it was designated Australia's capital. It's well situated, but a very small place. At first, building it up to the standard you'd expect of a capital city was a gold mine for anyone in the planning and construction businesses.'

'I imagine it was.'

'But no one had reckoned on Black Tuesday,' Claybourne continued. 'After the crash, the Australian economy took a dive and work on Canberra was put on hold.'

He paused and de Silva wondered if he should prompt him. A few moments elapsed before he resumed speaking. 'There was no point going there after that. I'd heard there was work in the gold mining area around Kalgoorlie, so I decided to try there instead. Ralph agreed to tag along and I was glad of his company.'

He pulled a packet of cigarettes from his pocket. 'Mind if I smoke?'

De Silva shook his head and waited while Claybourne lit up and dragged deeply on the cigarette.

'It was up there that we ran into Johnny. I never found out what line of work he was really in, but there was a lot of big talk about his theories of investment and how much money he'd made in the precious metals markets. In those parts, it was hard to tell just how wealthy people were. There was nowhere to spend money apart from in the hotels and bars and none of them exactly rivalled the Ritz. People mostly dressed in a rough-and-ready style and had little time for social distinctions.' He smiled dryly. 'That's something I've noticed Australians pride themselves on.'

De Silva rotated his pen between the fingers and thumb of one hand, wondering when this man was going to get to the point. He still wasn't sure what to make of him but decided to humour him for a while longer.

'Ralph had inherited money when his parents died. Not enough to keep him for the rest of his life, he needed to work, but enough to ensure that he and Helen would always be well off. Johnny soon found out about that and he also discovered Ralph had fancy relations back in England. He started calling him Lord Ralph. Ralph laughed but I knew he was embarrassed. Johnny kept telling him he should go and find the relations. There could be money in it. But Ralph was happy with the life he had in Australia. He wasn't interested in getting to know the grandfather who had kicked his father out, or the rest of the family who had stood by and watched it happen.'

'How long do you believe he'd known about his family history?'

'As far as I know, for many years.'

'And had his parents been dead long?'

Claybourne frowned. 'Several years, I think. Why do you ask?'

'No particular reason.'

Interesting. If Claybourne was telling the truth, it didn't tally with what Petrie had said about Wynne-Talbot's mother's recent deathbed revelations.

'What about Mrs Wynne-Talbot? Do you have any idea how she felt about her husband's friendship with this man?'

'Helen? At first, she used to complain to me about him all the time. But it wasn't long before I began to suspect that was just a smokescreen.'

Claybourne stubbed out the remains of his cigarette in the ashtray on de Silva's desk. 'I soon discovered I was right. They didn't bother to keep their affair secret for long. Ralph tried to pretend it wasn't happening but eventually he confronted Helen. She just laughed at him and refused to talk about it. Weeks turned into months and eventually Ralph confided in me. I tried to help, but there wasn't much to be done. Helen and Johnny were behaving completely brazenly by then.'

'Then why didn't her husband leave her?'

'He couldn't bring himself to. Ralph adored Helen. Even when anyone could see it was hopeless, he still clung onto the hope she'd come back to him.'

There was a knock at the door and Nadar looked in. 'Sir, excuse me, but you wanted me to remind you about that important meeting.'

De Silva waved a dismissive hand. 'It'll have to wait. Tell them I'll telephone later.'

Nadar looked surprised but he nodded and closed the door.

'It all came to a head at the end of '33,' Claybourne continued. 'It was New Year's Eve and the four of us had agreed to spend it together. Helen made up some story about a headache and wanting to rest first and said she'd join us later. Johnny also said he had business to attend to so Ralph and I should go on ahead. Ralph put a good face on it but he must have been suspicious. I wasn't. It was clear as day they planned to go somewhere together and wouldn't turn up.'

Claybourne fished the cigarette packet out of his pocket, extracted another one and lit it. De Silva was increasingly puzzled. By now the attention seekers he'd come across in Colombo had usually betrayed themselves with some wildly improbable claim or other. He remembered one who had been certain he had been visited by the ghost of Queen Victoria. Another had confided that the goddess Kali had entrusted him with the secret of a neighbour's imagined crime and instructed him to see that the man was punished. This man's speech and manner were, however, remarkably measured and calm.

'It was getting late and Ralph could hardly get his head off the table for whisky. I decided it was time to call a halt and get him back to the place where we were living.'

Claybourne fell silent once again, his eyes blank as if he had forgotten where he was. De Silva hesitated to prompt him.

'I don't believe the earthquake was reported outside Australia,' he continued at last. 'Quakes aren't an uncommon occurrence in the Western Territory. In any case,' he added grimly, 'the rest of the world tends not to take too much interest in what goes on down under.'

He paused again. The only sound in the room was the thrum of the ceiling fan blades chopping the heavy air. De Silva studied his silent visitor. What was he after? To discredit this Johnny Randall? If Wynne-Talbot really was dead and Randall was trying to usurp his life, unmasking him was going to be a very tricky task. Certainly not one to be undertaken lightly. Still, he'd give Claybourne a few more minutes. 'At times, we feel much the same in Ceylon,' he remarked. 'Please, go on.'

'As I said, Ralph was very drunk that night. I'm afraid that wasn't unusual by then. We'd got back to the room and he was still sleeping it off when the earthquake struck. It was a big one, and the mining town was close to the epicentre. I'd never experienced anything like it before and I hope never to again. The flophouse we were in was intact one minute and heaving and cracking the next.

'I managed to get Ralph up and drag him down the stairs. When we got outside, I vividly remember a big crack in the earth zigzagging along behind us as we ran down the street. Powerlines had ruptured and fires soon started to break out. Lethal when most of a town's built of wood. The weather had been dry for weeks and the flames jumped easily from one building to another until half the place was alight. We had fire trucks, but it took a while before people sobered up and started to bring them to where they were needed.

'Ralph got it into his head that he must find Helen. He wanted to be sure she was safe. He wouldn't listen to anything I said so all I could do was follow him. We ran into a few people we knew and one of them thought he'd seen Helen and Johnny going into the hotel where Johnny was staying. We got there to find there'd been a fire but it was mostly out and rescue workers were retrieving bodies. Johnny and Helen hadn't yet been found.'

De Silva noticed that the hand holding the cigarette trembled; the index and third fingers were stained yellowish-brown.

'Ralph grabbed one of the rescue workers and demanded to know if every floor had been searched. We knew Johnny and Helen had rooms on the top floor. The fellow said the staircase up to it was shot to pieces and they hadn't been able to get there.'

Claybourne stood up and went to the window. From the set of his shoulders, de Silva guessed he was trying to master his emotions. At last he went on in a rasping voice. 'I don't think I'll ever forget the stench in that building. Ralph dashed in before I had time to stop him. I followed, covering my face as well as I could to keep out the stink and the smoke, but my eyes were soon streaming. The wooden walls and beams were charred black and you couldn't trust that any board you stepped on wouldn't burn the shoes off your feet or give way under you and send you hurtling down to the floor below.

'We got as far as the last flight of stairs to the top floor and I saw what the fireman meant. There was just a skeleton structure left. Ralph started to claw his way up but what was left of it gave way under his weight. As he fell, I rushed towards him and tried to grab him. There was a terrible creaking and cracking and a bang like a charge going off down the mine, then something came down on my head and knocked me unconscious.'

There was a long pause. De Silva wasn't sure whether to believe a word of this, although if Claybourne was making it up, he had a vivid imagination and a knack for veracity. De Silva remembered a visit he'd once had to make to a crime scene in Colombo after an arson attack. Claybourne's description brought the scene back and he had to control the sick feeling in his stomach the memory still had the power to arouse.

'When I came round, I wasn't sure where I was. There was still a lot of gritty smoke in the air and it wasn't easy to see much. Something heavy lay across my back and my left leg, preventing me from moving. My head felt as if it would split, and something sticky, blood I suppose, trickled into my mouth. The pain was terrible, so bad it was hard to think about anything else. But I was aware of someone lying nearby. He was trapped under a pile of debris. It took me a while to realise who it was.'

'The man you say was Ralph Wynne-Talbot?'

'Yes,' said Claybourne bleakly. 'I wanted to call out to him, but when I tried to speak or move, the pain was too much. It was then I saw another man coming towards us. He was on his hands and knees, inching forward with great care. It was Johnny.'

He gave a harsh laugh. 'If I'd been able to attract his attention, I doubt I'd be here today telling you this. It's ironic that the pain I was in saved me. He got to Ralph and stopped but he didn't speak. I saw one of Ralph's hands lift a little and he made a low, guttural, moaning sound.'

He swallowed hard. De Silva watched the ash from the cigarette drop unheeded onto Claybourne's khaki trousers. 'What made me do it, I can't say, but I lowered my eyelids so I could only just see out and stayed very still. If Johnny planned to rescue us, it seemed strange he didn't speak. Wouldn't he want to know if we were alive before risking his own life? And if we were alive, wouldn't he want to reassure us? Instead, he ripped a piece from Ralph's shirt and I heard muffled sounds, as if Ralph was trying to speak. Then Johnny pressed the wad over Ralph's nose and mouth. The sounds faded. He struggled for a few moments, then he lay still.'

Claybourne's voice tailed away. The misery in his eyes stirred de Silva's pity. Even if the allegation was a massive fiction, it was excruciatingly real to this man. De Silva couldn't help shuddering himself at the thought of such a cold-blooded execution of a defenceless man.

'Would you like me to call for some tea, sir?' he asked quietly.

Claybourne shook his head. 'There's no need.' He moistened his dry lips with his tongue. 'People talk about being sick with fear and I never knew how that felt until that night. I waited to see what Johnny would do next. Even though the windows had been blown out with the heat, there wasn't much light, but if he saw me, I knew I was a dead man.' He gave a bitter smile. 'Some people might say what happened next was a stroke of luck and, in a way, I suppose it was. There was another creak and the floor moved. Johnny let out a yell and slid backwards. I heard other voices shouting to us, then I was falling, and again I lost consciousness.'

De Silva cleared his throat. He needed to bring the interview to a close and think this new information through.

'It seems you are lucky to be alive, Mr Claybourne, but you've told me you were in terrible pain and it was hard to see what was going on around you. Are you absolutely sure about what you think you saw?'

'I don't *think*, Inspector. I know what I saw.'

De Silva felt a wave of anger roll towards him from the other side of the desk but he was determined not to back down. Slowly, Claybourne mastered himself. 'I don't blame you for being sceptical. It's an extraordinary story.' His shoulders slumped and the next words were barely audible. 'All I ask is that you hear me out.'

'Of course.'

'Thank you.' Mechanically, he rubbed his left leg. 'I was taken to hospital,' he went on. 'Later I learnt that I had suffered a severe concussion, which explained why for a long time I remembered nothing, not even my own name. It was only after my memory started to return that everything that happened that night came back to me. I—'

A paroxysm of coughing prevented him from continuing. De Silva went to the door and called Nadar to bring some water. Claybourne gulped it gratefully. 'The smoke,' he said at last. 'The doctors told me my lungs would never be the same.'

No doubt the cigarettes didn't help, thought de Silva. 'So where did you go after your recovery?' he asked.

'When I left hospital, I was sent to convalesce at a place near Perth. Several months passed before I was fit enough to leave, but when I was, I learnt from police records that Ralph was dead. I'd also been recorded missing, presumed dead; a misconception I didn't chose to correct for a time.'

'What about Randall?'

'I could find no evidence of his death.'

'So, to sum up, you believe you saw him kill Mr Wynne-Talbot that night? Mr Claybourne, you're making a very serious accusation.'

'I appreciate that.'

'Putting it aside, if the man who claims to be Ralph Wynne-Talbot is Johnny Randall, how did you track him down to Ceylon?'

'When I'd fully recovered, I didn't want to stay in Australia but I wasn't sure I wanted to return to England either. The British government was advertising for engineers to work on the roads here and that seemed to be the answer. I work mostly in the north of the country but I happened to be down in Colombo for a meeting when the *Colombo Times* reported the arrival of Ralph Wynne-Talbot and his wife. One look at the photograph on the front page and I realised what Johnny was up to. It wasn't enough for him to step into Ralph's shoes with Helen, he wanted everything that was Ralph's by right.'

'Mr Claybourne, say you're right about this, and I'm afraid it will take more than your word alone to convince me, what do you believe Helen Wynne-Talbot knew about her husband's death?'

'She probably wasn't aware that Johnny's responsible, although of course she must have colluded with his impersonating Ralph. Helen was always the nervy type and pretty neurotic. I doubt Johnny would entrust her with his biggest secret. Even she might find it too much to stomach,' he added sourly.

De Silva's mind whirred. Was this story the truth or a carefully concocted pack of lies? For the moment, he could think of no more questions that might be useful – except perhaps one.

'Has engineering always been your field, Mr Claybourne?'

Claybourne's forehead puckered. 'Yes, but I'm puzzled as to why you ask.'

'No particular reason, sir. I'm just curious. Do I take it that the man you refer to as Ralph Wynne-Talbot had less experience than you?'

Claybourne looked faintly irritated. 'It stands to reason as Ralph was my junior. But don't misunderstand me, Inspector, he was a very capable engineer and loved his work. It was in his private life that he failed to succeed and that was through no fault of his own.'

De Silva rose to his feet. 'I'm afraid I must bring our discussion to a close for the moment, Mr Claybourne. I have other business to attend to. But please feel free to come back if you have anything further to tell me.'

He saw Claybourne's knuckles blanch. 'Do I understand you correctly? You have no intention of taking this matter any further? Are you satisfied that an innocent man is dead and the man who committed the crime can look forward to a life of wealth and privilege?'

De Silva maintained an impassive expression, refusing to rise to the bait. 'I'll make some enquiries,' he said, ignoring the fact that he hadn't the glimmer of an idea in what direction they might usefully lie.

'Ah, enquiries.'

'Yes. Is there somewhere I can reach you if I need to speak to you about the results?'

Claybourne got to his feet. 'Oh, I'll find you, Inspector. Rest assured of that.'

CHAPTER 24

The door closed and de Silva inhaled deeply then exhaled in a long, slow sigh. This was a development he could well have done without, but instinct told him he would be wrong to dismiss it out of hand. He remembered his motto: no stone unturned.

He looked at his watch. He knew Jane wasn't at home for lunch so he'd planned to ask Prasanna or Nadar to fetch him some food from one of the stalls in the bazaar, but now he changed his mind. A drive in the Morris always helped to clear his head; he'd go down to the lake for an hour. There were always plenty of food vendors there and after the long meeting he was hungry.

The calm waters of the town's large lake sparkled in the sunshine. It was a fine asset to Nuala and one the inhabitants didn't need to thank the British for. Like the majority of Ceylon's numerous lakes, it had been constructed in the time of the kings to conserve the precious water that reached the island twice a year in the form of the monsoons.

He parked the Morris at the edge of the grassy shore and pulled up the hood. There were several stalls nearby doing brisk business as well as vendors weaving among the groups of people who had, like himself, decided to spend their lunchtime by the lake. He purchased a round of naan bread, some dahl and a vegetable curry and found somewhere to sit.

Although he always teased Jane about her British addiction to travelling rugs, it might have been good to have one today. In spite of the recent rain, the ground was dry and dusty.

He took off his jacket and sat down. Breaking the naan into pieces, he used it to scoop the dahl and curry into his mouth. As he ate, he went over the conversation with Claybourne. Now that the man was no longer in front of him, his doubts increased, but what if the story was true? The implications were tremendous. He would have a murder case on his hands that threatened to shake British society in Ceylon and abroad.

His stomach gave a lurch. There was also the matter of Helen Wynne-Talbot. If there was murder involved, had she been an accomplice? Had her guilt become too much for her? Did it explain why she jumped? He would have to watch his step. It was all too easy to imagine how outraged Archie Clutterbuck would be if he made allegations that proved to be untrue, to say nothing of William Petrie...

A crow landed next to him, cocking its head and fixing its beady eyes on the remains of his lunch. De Silva wiped up the last of the curry and dahl but kept back a piece of naan before signalling to the vendor who waited nearby to take back the bowls. He stood up and stretched, then crumbled the remains of the naan and threw it for the crow. By the time he reached the Morris, a small flock had descended and were squabbling over the crumbs. Like the British would be over his carcass if he got this one wrong.

On his return to the station, he found the public room deserted. He picked up the bell on the counter and rang it briskly. A moment later, Constable Nadar appeared from the back looking flustered.

'Forgive me, sir, I wasn't gone for long.'

'I should hope not. Where's Prasanna?'

'In the backyard, sir.'

'What's he doing there?'

Nadar shifted his weight from one foot to the other. 'I'm not sure I should say, sir.'

De Silva's forehead puckered. 'You make it sound very serious, Constable.'

'It is, sir,' said Nadar unhappily, 'but I do not have any business telling you. Prasanna will be doing that himself.'

Mystified, de Silva walked down the short corridor that led to the backyard. As he drew near, a monotonous thumping noise reached him, coming at regular intervals, as if someone was hammering a piece of wood.

In the sunny yard, Prasanna was throwing a cricket ball hard against one of the walls then catching it on the rebound and hurling it again. De Silva watched him for a few throws before loudly clearing his throat. The ball fell to the ground and rolled away.

Prasanna's expression combined dejection and defiance; de Silva felt a prickle of disquiet. What had the young man been up to? He didn't speak, so de Silva was forced to break the silence.

'Out with it then, Sergeant. If you've made a mistake, I expect we can fix it.'

Prasanna shook his head. 'It's nothing like that, sir,' he mumbled, staring at the ground.

De Silva hesitated. If it was nothing to do with Prasanna's work, questions might be overly intrusive.

The sergeant looked up. 'I'm sorry, sir,' he said awkwardly. 'If you'll excuse me, I'll be getting back to work.'

'Very well.'

Puzzled, de Silva watched him go. Whatever it was, Prasanna clearly didn't want to talk about it and it was no use relying on Nadar to enlighten him. He sighed. He'd come to Nuala hoping for a quiet life; two mysteries in one day didn't sit well with that. He didn't relish the prospect of double trouble.

* * *

'You're very preoccupied, Shanti,' said Jane as they ate dinner that evening. On his drive home, he had resolved not to mention Claybourne to her. She might worry the man was a dangerous crank. Prasanna was another matter. He knew she had a soft spot for the likeable young sergeant.

'I'm sure it's true that it's nothing to do with his work,' she said when he told her what had happened that afternoon. 'He's a very decent young man. If something had gone wrong, I have no doubt he would own up. No, I'm convinced it's to do with this girl, Kuveni.'

De Silva rubbed his chin. 'I suppose I should have thought of that. He would be upset if he'd argued with his mother over her. Mrs Prasanna may be bossy but I know he's very fond of her and takes his filial duties seriously.'

'Well, if we're to help in some way, we need him to talk to us.'

De Silva pushed the remains of his dinner to the side of his plate, put down his knife and fork and nodded uncertainly.

Jane chuckled. 'Don't worry, dear. I'm not suggesting it has to be you.'

He brightened. 'You mean you'll speak to him? Why that's an excellent idea. You'll do a far better job of it than I ever could. Are you at home tomorrow?'

'I can be. There's plenty to be getting on with. I've promised Florence to make some things for the Bring and Buy stall at the fête. I thought it might be cancelled after poor Mrs Wynne-Talbot's death but Florence says Lady Caroline was adamant that life must go on as usual in Nuala, even though she's made her excuses and won't attend. Well, no one would expect her to after what's happened. I'm sure the last thing she wants is anyone fussing over her. Florence says the family intend to have a very quiet funeral, but

Reverend Peters may say a few words in church on Sunday.'

'Then tomorrow I'll think of an excuse to send Prasanna up here to fetch something for me.' He grinned. 'If I know you, you'll have him coughing up the beans in no time.'

CHAPTER 25

He arrived at the station the following morning to find a still-disconsolate Sergeant Prasanna talking quietly to Constable Nadar. Their conversation ceased abruptly at the sight of de Silva and they chorused a good morning.

'Anything new to report?'

'No, sir.' With Prasanna in such low spirits, there seemed to be a chance of Nadar becoming the spokesman for the two of them. The sergeant looked as if he hadn't slept well at all and the top button of his tunic was undone. In the circumstances, de Silva refrained from telling him off.

'I was halfway here when I realised I'd left some important papers at home,' he said. 'Prasanna, I'd like you to go and fetch them, please. Mrs de Silva will know where they are. If there's nothing urgent this morning, you may take your time over it.'

If Prasanna was surprised by this unusual request, it didn't disturb his listless expression. He merely nodded and got up from his seat behind the public counter.

Nadar, however, looked puzzled. 'What would you like me to do this morning, sir?' he asked as the door closed behind Prasanna.

'I need to go out for a few hours so you'd better hold the fort, Constable. If anyone asks for me, tell them I'll be back around lunchtime.'

Buoyed up by the conviction of a good job done, de Silva

emerged into the sunshine and climbed into the Morris. If he returned to the station at lunchtime, Prasanna would probably be back and he knew he could rely on Jane to sort out the problem in the meantime. What he wanted to do was find out where Claybourne was living. It would probably involve a morning, if not longer, of scouting round the hotels but it would be worth it. He disliked being ambushed and if he let the initiative remain with Claybourne that was very likely to be what happened next.

* * *

After she saw her husband off to work, Jane settled herself on the verandah with her work basket containing the embroidery silks she was using to make evening purses and spectacle cases for the Bring and Buy stall at the fête. As she sewed, she listened for the sound of Sergeant Prasanna's bicycle crunching over the gravel.

She didn't have to wait long; she was putting the finishing touches to a particularly pretty purse embroidered with flowers and bees on a pale-green background, when one of the servants came to the verandah door. 'The sergeant from the station is here, memsahib. He is asking if he may speak to you.'

'Of course he may. Will you ask him to come round by the garden?'

'Yes, memsahib.'

She made a show of looking surprised as Prasanna came up the steps, his cap in his hand. 'I'm sorry to disturb you, ma'am, but Inspector de Silva has sent me to fetch some important papers he left behind this morning. He says you will know where they are.'

Tutting, Jane put her sewing aside and smiled at him. 'How good of you to come all this way, Sergeant, and how forgetful my husband is becoming. I hope you aren't in a hurry?'

'No, ma'am, Inspector de Silva said I do not need to be back urgently.'

'Good, because although I have some idea where the papers are, it may take me a little while to find them. Won't you sit down and have a cold drink while you wait? You must be very warm after cycling all the way up from town.'

Prasanna looked doubtful. 'I don't want to be in your way, ma'am. I can wait in the kitchen.'

'Nonsense, you won't be in my way and it's far too lovely a morning to be indoors. I'll go and find the papers and in the meantime one of the servants will prepare us some iced tea.'

Inside the bungalow, Jane went to the study. She collected up a few old car magazines, put them in a large envelope and sealed the flap. What a lot of these magazines Shanti had. She'd have to speak to him about sorting them out and getting rid of some of them. But then again, she had a considerable pile of film magazines. Perhaps they should both go through and pick out the ones they would never look at again. They might fetch a few pence on the Bring and Buy stall.

In her neat, teacher's hand, she wrote the words, "For the attention of Inspector de Silva. Most urgent." on the envelope then waited until she heard the footsteps of the servant she had instructed to take tea to the verandah before returning to Prasanna.

The young man leapt to his feet and smiled shyly. 'This is very kind of you, ma'am.'

'Not at all. I usually have a little something at about this time and I'm delighted to have company to share it with. Now, do sit down. You must try a slice of our cook's butter cake. He makes a very good one.'

They sat down and he took a piece of the cake and put

it on his plate. 'I have been admiring your sewing, ma'am.'

'Oh, I'm not very skilled but I enjoy it and it passes the time.' She held up the purse. 'I'm making this for one of the stalls at the church fête that's coming up soon. It's the kind of thing that always sells well. I only wish I had time to make more but I fear I'm a very slow needlewoman. Does your mother like to sew, Sergeant Prasanna?'

A glum expression clouded Prasanna's face. 'No, ma'am.'

'What a pity. Well, if you should happen to think of anyone who might like to give me some help, it's for a very good cause. We hope to raise money for orphaned children of the plantation workers.'

'As you say, ma'am, a very good cause.' He paused, bestowing a dejected look on the crumbs on his plate.

'Do have another piece,' Jane said encouragingly, pointing to the cake stand. He took a slice but instead of eating it, began crumbling it absentmindedly.

'*Have* you someone in mind, Sergeant?' she asked gently.

He looked up. 'I have a friend who is very clever with her needle, but she will not be in Nuala much longer.'

'Oh dear, what a pity. Are you sure she can't be prevailed upon to stay, just for a little while?'

Prasanna reduced the cake to dust. 'No, ma'am.' He rubbed his eyes. 'It is impossible.'

'Nothing is impossible, Sergeant. Perhaps if you tell me more, I will be able to help. I have, after all, lived a great many more years than you.'

Jane watched him avert his eyes and felt a pang of annoyance with herself. Had she taken too much of a liberty and lost her chance of winning his confidence? His next words, however, reassured her.

'Mrs de Silva... I would be very grateful if you would help me.'

'And I'll be delighted to do whatever I can.'

'Inspector de Silva has been so good to me that I don't know how to tell him.'

There was a long pause. 'Tell him what, Sergeant?' asked Jane eventually.

'I must leave the police force, ma'am.'

'Gracious me, that seems very drastic. Surely there is some other way of dealing with this problem, whatever it is? My husband is always telling me he thinks you have the ability to go far. It would be a great pity to give up now.'

Prasanna chewed his lower lip. 'He is very kind to say so, ma'am, but there is no other way.'

'Sergeant, does this have something to do with a young lady called Kuveni?'

Prasanna looked sheepish. 'Yes, ma'am.'

A defiant look came into his eyes. 'We want to be together and that is impossible if I stay. Her father is sicker and sicker every day and her brother, Vijay, wants to take him back to the jungle. He refuses to leave his sister alone in Nuala so she must go too. They will not come back here. Vijay claims it is living among so many people in a town that has made their father ill in the first place. He believes that returning to the old Vedda ways is the only thing that will cure him.'

'But it may not be the right thing for Kuveni?'

'I'm sure of that, but she does not want to disobey her father and her brother. The only answer is for me to hand in my notice and go with them.' He averted his eyes. 'I still have to tell my mother what I have decided. She will not like it but it can't be helped.'

Jane's forehead creased. 'Oh dear, my husband will be very sorry and so shall I. To say nothing of how your poor mother will feel. Surely if we put our heads together, we can solve the problem?'

Prasanna looked bemused and she smiled. 'I mean that between the two of us, we should be able to find a solution to your problem.'

'You are very kind to say so, ma'am, but I do not think any other way is possible.'

She studied him pensively. 'Do you know something, Sergeant? I believe you may be wrong about that.'

CHAPTER 26

'By golly, when you said you would speak to Prasanna I didn't expect everything to be settled so quickly.'

'I didn't see a good reason to delay. Kuveni and her family might have left Nuala at any moment and then where would we have been?'

'Where indeed. I know that I would have been very sorry to lose my sergeant.'

De Silva stretched his legs out on the hearthrug and took a sip of his whisky and soda. It had been a tiring day and he felt he had earned a strong one. He still hadn't managed to track down Matthew Claybourne, and all he had to show for his exertions was sore feet. The thought of losing his promising sergeant was even more disturbing than it might otherwise have been. 'So you've already seen the girl and her family and they agree to her coming to live here, as we discussed?'

'Yes. Her father and her brother were a little dubious at first but I managed to reassure them.' She chuckled. 'Kuveni herself needed very little persuasion. It's clear to me she's as fond of Prasanna as he is of her. She was happy with the idea of helping me with the sewing and after the fête is over, I'm sure I can find plenty of other little jobs for her to do for as long as she wants to stay. As you said, she seems very bright. We shall see what can be achieved with a few English lessons. If she learns to speak the language, it will open many doors.'

De Silva's head was in a whirl. He knew from experience that once Jane seized on a plan, there was no stopping her. He thought, however, that he ought to introduce a note of caution. 'But what about Prasanna's mother? Suppose she remains opposed to the match? We don't want to come between her and her son, do we?'

'Of course not, but I'm confident that once she's acquainted with Kuveni and sees how she and Prasanna feel about each other, she'll give them her blessing.'

He leant across and patted her knee. 'Congratulations, my love. Mrs Bennet was an amateur compared to you.'

'You know, dear, I rather think she was.'

* * *

The days that followed passed peacefully. In fact so peacefully that de Silva put thoughts of his perplexing visitor to the back of his mind. They only returned to Claybourne when he heard that, with the funeral now over, Lady Caroline and Ralph Wynne-Talbot would shortly leave Nuala for Colombo and the ship for England. If Claybourne didn't return soon, Wynne-Talbot would be five thousand miles away and safely installed as the 14th Earl of Axford. It would be far too late to challenge him then.

De Silva added some more curlicues to the doodle on his blotter as he mulled the matter over. It went against his principles to give up, and Claybourne's story hung together, but what else could he do? Confronting Ralph Wynne-Talbot with an accusation of murder was going to be risky enough, but when it was solely based on the evidence of someone who had vanished into thin air, it was professional suicide.

The pen inscribed a final flourish; he replaced the cap and looked at the clock. Good, it was time to shut the station and go home. As the Morris purred towards Sunnybank, he looked forward to a pleasant evening with Jane.

* * *

'Much more of this whistling around the station and Nadar and I will have to stuff a gag in Prasanna's mouth,' he remarked as he and Jane ate dinner. 'I'm not sure it wasn't better when he was behaving like a wet month.'

'A wet weekend, dear, and I'm sure you don't mean it.'

He grinned. 'I'm joking, of course. But it did seem more like a month than a weekend.'

'And what about Constable Nadar? I hope the baby isn't still teething.'

'I believe that is over and for the present Nadar is remarkably alert. Do you know, I believe life in Nuala may be measuring up to expectations after all?'

'We mustn't tempt fate, but you may be right. It's nice to have nothing more to worry about than whether the fête will go well on Saturday.'

'Of course it will. I feel it in my bones.'

He helped himself to spicy dahl and a large spoon of fragrant rice. 'How is the sewing getting on?'

'Very well. Kuveni is so much quicker than I am and has lots of good ideas for designs. I think Florence can't fail to be impressed and that will be a very good thing. If I let her believe that Kuveni is her own discovery, she'll recommend her to her friends. Kuveni might build up a nice little business given time.'

'That's excellent. So even if things don't work out between her and my sergeant, she has a skill that will enable her to support herself.'

Jane looked at him quizzically. 'Oh, I don't think we need worry about that.'

She put down her knife and fork and replaced her napkin in its silver ring. 'I think I shall read for an hour or two. I need a rest from all this sewing.'

'I'll join you, but I'd like a walk round the garden first.'

'Well, be careful not to bump into anything.'

'You know I have the eyes of an owl.'

The balmy night air intensified the scents in the garden. De Silva loved to walk among the flowerbeds at this time, drinking in the many aromas and admiring how the moonlight cloaked everything with a silvery sheen. Small scuffling sounds in the bushes told him he wasn't alone. He heard the high-pitched squeak of fruit bats on their nightly hunt.

Then all at once, there was a different sound from the direction of the large tulip tree, as if a bigger creature had found its way into the garden. He froze and listened; it might be many things. Monkeys, or perhaps one of the big monitor lizards, even – and the thought caused him considerable alarm – a leopard that had wandered out of the jungle in search of easy prey. Most wild animals would do you no harm unless you cornered them and he had no intention of doing that, but a leopard might be hungry.

Very cautiously, he crept across the lawn in the direction of the verandah. His heart pumped faster and the blood sang in his ears as he thought he saw something move behind a tree. Was there a low snarl too? He kept moving slowly; it was a mistake to run. A leopard had the speed to outrun the Morris, let alone a middle-aged policeman who was a little too fond of his food.

In the drawing room's lighted window he saw Jane already settled in her chair, her head bent over her book. A few more moments and he reached the verandah and slipped inside to join her, closing the door firmly behind him.

Jane looked up. 'Whatever's the matter, dear? You look quite unnerved.'

'I believe we have an intruder in the garden. A leopard possibly.'

'Gracious. Isn't it unusual for them to come so close?'

'Yes, but maybe it's an old one and not as fast as it was. Domestic animals are attractive then.'

Jane shuddered. 'They're such beautiful creatures but I prefer not to share the garden with one.'

He picked up his book. 'Don't worry. In the morning, I'll get the gardener to check all the fences.' It was only later that it occurred to him that the interloper might have been human.

CHAPTER 27

For as long as anyone could remember, the Nuala church fête had been held in the garden at the vicarage. This year was no exception and, as de Silva carried boxes and bags to the trestles set up ready for the Bring and Buy stall, he glanced at the roses and felt mischievously gratified that his were, once again, doing far better than the vicar's.

He put down the last of the boxes and wiped his forehead with his handkerchief. 'Phew! Perhaps I was a beast of burden in a former life but I hope I won't have to be one again.'

'Poor dear. There's a refreshment stall over there in the shade. Why don't you fetch yourself a cold drink?'

'I might just do that. Would you like something too?'

'Not yet, thank you. I'd rather set everything up first and I expect the others will be here any moment. I'm expecting Kuveni as well. She's coming by rickshaw with a few last-minute things.'

'So it sounds as if you won't be needing me on the stall then.'

'Probably not, but I forgot to mention that Joan Buscott's husband would be very grateful for some help with the Pin the Tail on the Donkey competition and the coconut shy. He's such a nice man; I'm sure you'll enjoy chatting with him.'

'Fine. I'll get something to drink first then go and introduce myself.'

There were several ladies busying about at the refreshment stall. Among them, de Silva noticed Reverend Peters' wife, second-in-command to Florence Clutterbuck in Nuala's social hierarchy. She broke off from what she was doing to exchange a few civil words with him and he paid for and drank his lemonade. Plates filled with tempting-looking cakes and biscuits were already laid out under net covers to keep away flies. He made a mental note to return later.

Joan Buscott's husband was hammering a square white post into the ground when de Silva reached the coconut shy. Shading his eyes with one hand, he stopped work for a moment. A tall man with an enviably luxuriant head of greying hair, he had bushy eyebrows that reminded de Silva of the fat caterpillars he had removed from one of his chrysanthemums on his walk round the garden at Sunnybank that morning.

'Ah, Inspector de Silva, I presume! Good of you to help out. I've got Doctor Hebden coming along later but he has a patient to attend to first.' He extended a leathery hand. 'John Buscott, by the way.'

Between them, they soon had the rest of the posts in place and coconuts balanced on the top of each one. Prizes were laid out and the venerable cork board set up with a picture of a grey donkey pinned to it. Buscott fished around in a box and found the tail. 'Excellent,' he said, putting it on the table next to the blindfold. 'All shipshape and Bristol fashion. Now we can settle down for a bit and wait for the fun to begin.'

He sat down and crossed one long leg over the other. The red-and-white striped deckchair gave a small creak of protest. 'This will be my last fête in Nuala,' he remarked.

'Ah yes, your wife mentioned at the Residence dinner that you are retiring back to England soon.'

Buscott nodded. 'We're not getting any younger and my

wife wants to be near our children and grandchildren. She's not had much time with the family what with following me round the world for most of my working life.' He pulled a packet of Passing Clouds out of his pocket – the same brand Archie Clutterbuck smoked, observed de Silva – and offered one. De Silva shook his head. 'Thank you, sir, but I won't.'

'Not a smoker, eh?'

'No.'

He excused himself the little white lie. The cigarette he'd smoked a few days ago had been medicinal. Now that everything was back to normal, he could do without one.

'Nice little seaside place called Broadstairs,' Buscott continued. 'That's where my wife's chosen. It's near the family and she loves the sea. I've toyed with the idea of taking up sailing again, used to be keen as a young man, but it's probably safest to concentrate on brushing up my golf swing. That's what my wife advocates anyway, and the ladies usually know best.'

'Indeed they do.'

'We'll be sad to leave, of course. It's been a good life here and an interesting one.'

'I understand you're an engineer?'

'That's right, man and boy. Railways mainly, so of course there's been plenty to keep me busy in Ceylon. I moved to the administrative side in my early fifties. Much as I enjoyed it, working in the field's a young man's game. My wife tells me you moved up here from Colombo for similar reasons.'

'Yes, I wanted a quieter pace of life.'

Conversation languished as Buscott puffed on his cigarette and they watched the trickle of early arrivals to the garden. 'I hear Lady Caroline won't be attending today,' Buscott remarked after a while. 'I think my wife was disappointed. They're old friends. But it's understandable. Terrible business about that niece of hers.'

'Terrible.'

'I suppose the nephew will rally, he has youth on his side, but that kind of thing knocks a man about a bit. Never really got to talk to him as much as I'd have liked. I'd hoped to hear about his involvement with the Sydney Harbour Bridge. Quite a feather in the old cap being associated with a project of that magnitude, but he wasn't very forthcoming when I asked him about it at the Clutterbucks' dinner. I suppose he had a lot on his mind even then. Probably shouldn't have expected him to spare the time to talk shop with an old buffer.'

He looked up. 'Ah, here come the hordes. Right de Silva, best foot forward!'

Best foot indeed, thought de Silva as he umpired excited children and gimlet-eyed fathers. An hour passed before David Hebden arrived, dressed in the ubiquitous cream linen suit and Panama hat of the Englishman abroad.

'Sorry not to be here before,' he said, shaking hands with Buscott. 'I'd promised to call in on one of my patients down near Hatton.'

He gave de Silva a curt nod and the inspector was taken aback. This was very odd. Even if their past history had not always run smoothly, their last meeting at the Clutterbucks' dinner had been perfectly amicable.

'That's quite alright,' said Buscott cheerfully, apparently oblivious to the awkwardness between his companions. 'Duty first, eh? Good to have you here now.' He gestured to the queue. 'As you see, we're a popular attraction. You might like to start by finding my wife and asking her if she's got anything extra tucked up her sleeve that we might use for prizes. We're in danger of running short.'

'Certainly.'

'Decent chap, Hebden,' Buscott observed as the doctor walked away to find Joan Buscott. 'Sound too, but unfortunately he wasn't able to help Mrs Wynne-Talbot.'

De Silva's ears pricked up. So that was it. He'd presumed that Hebden had told him in strict confidence about Ralph Wynne-Talbot's visit to him and he had respected that confidence, but Buscott's remark opened up a can of worms. How many other people knew of the visit and from whom had they learnt of it? And more to the point, who did Hebden think had talked out of turn?

Buscott's attention was diverted by the need to find a prize for a little boy who had just dislodged a coconut with each of the five balls his father had paid for. 'I think we've made it too easy,' he sighed when he returned. 'Ah, capital! Here comes Hebden with reinforcements.'

The queue dwindled as teatime approached and people descended on the refreshment tent. Buscott mopped his brow with a large white handkerchief. 'Tea be damned,' he said. 'I need a proper drink. Beer, gentlemen?'

Hebden nodded. 'Excellent idea.'

'What about you, de Silva?'

Although de Silva had developed a taste for whisky, beer was a beverage whose appeal still eluded him. 'I would prefer lemonade, if you don't mind. Shall I come and help you?' he added, not keen to be left alone with Hebden.

'No need, I can manage three glasses. You and Hebden keep an eye on things here.'

As Buscott went off in the direction of the refreshment tent, de Silva wondered what he should say. Hebden was bound to be offended if he thought that people in Nuala were questioning his professional ability. If he believed de Silva was the source of the story, he would inevitably direct his anger at him. One option was to say nothing and hope any animosity Hebden bore him would blow over. On the other hand, it would be interesting to know how Buscott had learnt that Hebden had been consulted over Helen Wynne-Talbot.

Hesitantly, he glanced sideways and found the doctor's grey eyes studying him grimly. There was no point dissembling.

'Please believe me when I say that I've never spoken to anyone of what you told me about Mr Wynne-Talbot's visit to you. And even though I trust her with my life to be discreet, I include my wife in that.'

Hebden didn't answer for a moment and de Silva's pulse quickened. At last the doctor nodded. 'Thank you, but I'm afraid someone did talk.' He thrust out his chin. 'Nevertheless, I stand by the advice I gave Wynne-Talbot. Tragic as the outcome was, his wife would have been no better off if I'd agreed to prescribe the drug he wanted. In fact it might even have increased her sufferings with the side-effects it causes.'

'Which are?'

'What he asked me for was a drug called Nembutal – a barbiturate. Among other things, it's used for the treatment of anxiety and insomnia. In small doses it induces a feeling of wellbeing and sociability in the same way that alcohol does. Increase the dose, however, even by a small margin, and the patient becomes hostile, irritable and frequently exhausted. Co-ordination is impaired, falls and accidents become a grave risk. A patient may suffer from hallucinations. In this confusion, the risk of a fatal overdose is also high.'

'In other words, a drug to be approached with great caution.'

'Absolutely. I wouldn't want a patient of mine prescribed it unless they were under continuing medical supervision.'

'So if people were somehow given the impression that you refused to help Mrs Wynne-Talbot, even though there was a viable treatment available, that would be misleading?'

'Extremely misleading.'

Hebden's brow furrowed. 'If it wasn't you, de Silva and, I

hasten to add, I accept your assurance, who was it? I've had comments from all kinds of quarters, most of them harmless enough but I don't like it. The trust between doctor and patient is meant to be sacrosanct.'

De Silva looked up and saw John Buscott coming across the lawn with two glass tankards of India Pale Ale and a tall glass of lemonade.

'Enough said for the moment,' Hebden muttered. 'I suppose Buscott knows too?'

'I'm afraid so.'

An interesting exchange, de Silva thought as he sipped his lemonade and listened to the two Englishmen discuss cricket scores. If the opportunity arose, he'd like to find out where John Buscott had got his information from. It was also tempting to speculate why Ralph Wynne-Talbot hadn't wanted to talk to the older engineer about the Sydney Harbour Bridge. Was it simply because he didn't have the time, or was there more to it than that?

The afternoon drew to a close and people started to drift away. De Silva helped to dismantle the coconut shy and the donkey then went to find Jane who greeted him with a broad smile.

'You look as if you've had a better time of it than I have,' he said quietly.

'What do you mean?'

De Silva cast a glance at the other ladies still packing up unsold items and put a finger to his lips. 'I'll explain on the way home.'

'So what happened?' asked Jane as the Morris bowled along in the direction of Sunnybank.

'Buscott was no problem. It was Hebden.'

'Doctor Hebden? But he seems such a charming man.'

De Silva frowned. 'There's something I didn't tell you about Ralph Wynne-Talbot. Something Hebden told me in strict confidence. I suppose he thought he could trust me as I'm a policeman and, of course, if I had questioned him formally, he would have been obliged to tell me. Anyway, I kept the information to myself, then, to be perfectly honest, I forgot about it.'

'Go on.'

'Wynne-Talbot came to see Hebden a few days before his wife's death, asking him to prescribe a drug called Nembutal.'

Jane nodded. 'I've read about it. It's for the treatment of depression, isn't it?'

'Yes. Where did you hear about it?'

'I forget. It might have been an article in one of my film magazines.' She thought for a moment. 'Yes, that was it. There was a film made in America about a doctor who illicitly experimented on his patients with different drugs and it was one of them.'

'Well, the point is, Hebden declined to prescribe it because he thinks it often does more harm than good.'

'That does rather bear out what I believe happened in the film.'

'Wynne-Talbot apparently accepted his decision and that would have been the end of it except somehow word of their meeting got out.'

'Surely you didn't say anything, dear?'

'Certainly not, but there was a bit of an awkward moment while Hebden thought I was the one to blame. Luckily, he accepted my word that I wasn't.'

'I should hope so too. But who do you think it was?'

'I've no idea. John Buscott mentioned it while we were waiting for Hebden to arrive but I didn't have the chance to find out how he knew.'

'That's easy. I'm sure I can make discreet enquiries. I'll see Joan tomorrow. She and I are going to the orphanage with Florence Clutterbuck. We need to take them the money we made at the fête.'

'It might be very useful if you can find out.'

Jane tilted her head to one side. 'Does this mean you think there's something suspicious about Ralph Wynne-Talbot asking for Nembutal? It could have been perfectly innocent, you know. After all, he's not a medical man so he might not be aware of the disadvantages. In any case, he didn't get his prescription and you said he didn't argue with Doctor Hebden about that.'

'I agree that there may be nothing in it, but you know me.'

'I do, my dear. Never leave any stone unturned.'

'So tell me about your afternoon. Why so cheerful?'

'I do believe I've made a little bit of progress with Sergeant Prasanna's problem.'

'Really? That is good news.'

'I saw his mother near the stall looking as if she wanted to come over.'

'And did she?'

'After a while, yes. She thumbed through those film magazines I donated. Except I was sure she was only pretending to read them. I went over and talked to her. The atmosphere was rather awkward at first, but I'm convinced it was all a ploy. She wants to find out more about Kuveni.'

'How could you tell?'

'Female intuition, dear.'

'Ah.'

'I suddenly had an idea, so I steered the conversation round to the orphanage.'

'You're going too fast for me.' De Silva grinned, amused by his wife's energetic tone. 'Why did you do that?'

'Because it occurred to me that I might be able to interest her in doing some kind of event to help us with raising money. An afternoon of beauty treatments or demonstrations perhaps, I'd need to work out the details. Anyway, that's not so important. What is, is that she's coming to have tea with me to talk about it.'

'And Kuveni will be there?'

Jane beamed triumphantly. 'Of course, and once Mrs Prasanna gets to know her better, I'm certain she'll take a favourable view of her son's choice.'

He laughed. 'My head is in a whirl with all this matchmaking.'

'But you do think it will work, don't you?' she asked, suddenly anxious.

The Morris turned into the drive at Sunnybank and came to a stop at the front door. He applied the handbrake then leant across to kiss her cheek. 'It sounds like an excellent plan. Well done, my love.'

CHAPTER 28

At breakfast on the Monday morning, de Silva found an envelope beside his plate. It was much too early for the post to have been delivered. 'Where did this come from?' he asked the servant who brought his eggs.

'It was on the front door mat at dawn, sahib. No one saw the messenger.'

'Strange.' He looked at his plate. 'Good, the yolks are still soft. You can bring my coffee now, but tell Cook not to send the memsahib's eggs out yet, she won't be ready for another ten minutes at least.'

'Yes, sahib.'

The door closed behind the servant and de Silva slit the envelope with his knife – Jane would tell him off for that. He took out the letter and scanned it quickly then folded it up again and put it and the envelope in his pocket. How to deal with this? He wasn't sure yet. He picked up his knife and fork and attacked his eggs on toast.

* * *

The commotion at the police station greeted him the moment he walked through the door. A perspiring Constable Nadar looked up with palpable relief at the sight of him, and the two irate, gesticulating men in front of the desk, surrounded by their noisy gangs of supporters, fell to grumbling quietly.

'What's going on, Constable?' asked de Silva, ignoring them all for the moment. Nadar started to speak but, finding a second wind, the crowd started talking and shouting once again. De Silva raised a hand. 'Silence! Or I'll have the lot of you thrown out.'

With resentful looks, the crowd went quiet. De Silva pointed to the main protagonists. 'The two of you may come into my office. Nadar, show the rest the door.'

'Yes, sir.'

The two men trooped into the office behind de Silva and stood with downcast eyes while he settled himself behind his desk and took up paper and pen. 'Now, what's this all about?'

'He let his bullock knock over my stall. Everything is ruined – mangoes, bananas, everything. Nothing can be sold – all trampled in the dust.'

'He lies! And he has lost nothing worth selling anyway. It was all rotting produce no one wanted. Nothing else was touched.'

The first man lunged at his adversary's throat. 'I do not lie,' he hissed.

De Silva brought his fist down hard on the desktop. 'Enough!'

Both of the men stopped, resentful expressions on their faces. 'I'll come and see for myself,' said de Silva. 'Wait for me outside.' Muttering, the men went out to the public room and de Silva waited for a few minutes before following them. It would do them no harm to have a little time to cool off. He took out the letter that had been delivered that morning and read it once more then put it in one of his desk drawers. Perhaps it was as well that he didn't have time to decide how to act on it straight away. He'd think about it when this squabble was resolved.

'What a morning,' he said when he returned home for lunch. 'At one point the whole bazaar must have been involved and of course everyone had an opinion.'

'Really, dear? What was the matter?'

'Oh, a bullock ran amok and turned over a fruit and vegetable seller's stall. The bullock's owner was denying the damaged goods were worth anything.'

'Did you manage to resolve it?'

'After an hour or so, but it was hard going and I'm not sure either of them are really satisfied. Still, it can't be helped.'

'What a pity. Come and have your lunch. Cook has made your favourite.'

He rubbed his hands together. 'Pea and cashew curry. Just what the doctor ordered.'

'By the way,' said Jane as they ate. 'I managed to find out what you wanted to know about Ralph Wynne-Talbot and Doctor Hebden.'

'That didn't take you long.'

'It was easy. Joan Buscott's a charming lady but she doesn't have a suspicious bone in her body. Apparently she heard it from Florence and told her husband.'

'And did you find out who Florence heard it from?'

Jane gave him a triumphant smile. 'I did. It was from Ralph Wynne-Talbot himself.'

De Silva gave a low whistle.

'It does seem odd, doesn't it? But then after the tragedy he's suffered, perhaps he needed to prove to himself and everyone else that he did everything he could to prevent it.'

'Yes, I suppose that's it.' He scooped up the last of his curry and rice and ate it then pushed the plate away. 'Delicious.'

'Will you have some more?'

'Better not.' He patted his stomach.

'How sensible of you, my dear. Can you stay for a while?'

'No, I'd better get back. I've paperwork that needs dealing with and this morning held me up. Oh, I forgot to tell you, I'll be late home this evening. I have to see someone down in Hatton, so don't keep dinner waiting for me.'

'Alright, dear.'

As he went out to the Morris, he felt guilty about not telling her the truth but it was better that way. Nevertheless, a knot tightened in his stomach.

At the station, Nadar was alone. De Silva frowned. 'I don't recall sending Prasanna out for anything today. Where is he?'

Nadar fiddled with a pencil. 'He didn't come in, sir.'

'Why not?'

'I think he has some problems, sir...'

De Silva's frown deepened. If Prasanna and Kuveni had argued, surely Jane would have known about it?

'It is his aunties, sir. They tell him he will be the death of his mother and he must mend his ways.'

So that was it. To be frank, he was surprised this hadn't happened sooner. He hesitated: best not to mention Jane's scheme to Nadar for the moment. 'Hmm. In the circumstances, if you see him, you may tell him I excuse him today, but I expect him in the morning.'

'Yes, sir,' said Nadar unhappily.

In his office, de Silva took the letter from his drawer and studied the hand-drawn map and brief instructions one more time. Jane's news clinched it; Ralph Wynne-Talbot's admission might have been the outpouring of a troubled mind but it might have been less innocent. He had to know for sure. Distractedly, he applied himself to his paperwork. There were several hours to go before the rendezvous.

CHAPTER 29

Matthew Claybourne waited for him at an unremarkable guest house on the road that led north out of Nuala. De Silva wasn't surprised he hadn't thought to search it before. He found a place where the Morris wouldn't be too conspicuous and promised the guest house owner a generous tip to keep an eye on it.

They took Claybourne's car and drove for half an hour until the road became too broken up to go on. Setting off on foot, de Silva felt uneasy. There had been rain the previous night and the reddish-coloured mud on the narrow track soon coated his shoes and the bottoms of his uniform trouser legs. The trees crowded in on them, the smell of humid, burgeoning vegetation mingling unpleasantly with the stench of decay. A film of sweat soon covered his face and a million microscopic insects made the air hum with the vibration of their wings.

A nasty suspicion grew in his mind that Johnny Randall – if that was who the man calling himself Ralph Wynne-Talbot really was – would not show up. Realistically, he held all the cards. Even if there was truth in Claybourne's accusation, William Petrie and Archie Clutterbuck were unlikely to believe him. If I were in Wynne-Talbot's place, thought de Silva, I'd keep away and, if necessary, deny everything and rely on people thinking Claybourne was a crank, and a malicious one at that.

He yelped as, preoccupied with his thoughts, he stumbled over a tangle of roots snaking across the path.

'What was that?' asked Claybourne sharply.

'I tripped over one of these damned roots.'

'You'd better be more careful. I'm not planning on carrying you if you break anything.'

De Silva's fists clenched then he reminded himself of his resolve. They had started and, whatever the hazards, he would finish this crazy expedition. If it proved a waste of time and Claybourne still wouldn't see sense, he'd arrest him for wasting police time.

By the time they reached the spot where the jungle thinned, the sun was slipping below the tree canopy. It grew harder to see the way, but de Silva realised they were walking through what remained of an old coffee plantation. The area once under cultivation looked to have been quite small – a reminder that not all the planters who had come to Ceylon had been wealthy men.

In places, skeletons of coffee bushes clawed up from the brushwood and weeds, desolate evidence of *Hemileia vastatrix*. Coffee rust: or as it was more commonly known, Devastating Emily. The terrible blight had ravaged the coffee fields nearly seventy years ago, in most cases bankrupting those who had previously profited from Ceylon's fragrant black gold. It had taken years for the hill country to recover as the more tenacious planters developed the tea trade.

They headed for a low, L-shaped building in an advanced state of dilapidation that crouched at the western end of the fields. Even in the fast-fading light, the years of neglect were all too evident. Much of the roof had fallen in and through gaping holes, trees thrust their way to the sky. There was no glass in the windows but most of the bars fixed across them to deter burglars still looked intact.

De Silva followed Claybourne up the wooden steps to

the porch. The front door hung precariously by a single hinge. It opened with difficulty, making a grating sound that set de Silva's teeth on edge.

The room they walked into stank of damp; rubbish and dead leaves littered the floor. The remains of a meal stood on a table: a few scraps of bread and a melon rind that were providing a feast for a pair of common tiger butterflies. Through a door to the right, he caught a glimpse of a dimly lit room with a low bed in it. From the rumpled covers, it seemed that Claybourne had been sleeping in this godforsaken hole.

'How did you find this place?' asked de Silva.

'I spoke to some of the locals; they knew about it. I come here sometimes when I want some peace and quiet.'

'You certainly found it. What do you do for water and supplies?'

'There's a well at the back. As for the rest, I pay a local man to bring in what little I need.'

De Silva shuddered inwardly. How cheerless and lonely the place was. It was no wonder the fellow looked so grim.

'I don't expect Randall will be here for a while,' said Claybourne. 'I told the guide what time we would arrive and stressed that we wanted to be here first.'

'Always an advantage.' Surreptitiously, de Silva touched the Webley in the shoulder holster tucked under his jacket. If it came to a fight, he hoped the gun would be an advantage too.

Claybourne permitted himself a rare smile. 'I thought we might be glad of something to steady our nerves before the fun begins.' He went to a cupboard made of dry, cracked, wooden panels. The shelves held a meagre stock of packets and tins of food as well as a few mismatched tumblers and a bottle of whisky. Claybourne poured them each a generous measure then gestured to the verandah. 'It's stuffy in here. We can probably risk staying outside while we drink these.'

There was no furniture on the small verandah so they remained standing while they drank in silence. De Silva ran their agreement over in his mind. He was to conceal himself in the bungalow while Claybourne offered to throw in his lot with Randall. Claybourne was convinced that Randall would then say enough to incriminate himself and de Silva would pounce.

But a chill crept down de Silva's spine. Was he mad to have agreed to this? He imagined the scene if he'd been duped and had to explain that to Petrie and Clutterbuck.

Claybourne drained his glass and set it on the ground. 'Drink up. We'd better get ready for our visitor.'

The last of de Silva's whisky was still in his mouth when the blow hit him squarely in the diaphragm. With a gasp, he doubled over and alcohol splattered the boards. The glass dropped from his hand and shattered. He just had time to lift his head when Claybourne punched him again, this time between the eyes.

His legs gave way and the floor rushed up to meet him. Through a fog of pain, he realised that Claybourne had grabbed his wrists and pulled his hands behind his back. He tottered, blinking as he felt the sticky warmth of blood. A length of coarse rope went round his wrists, binding them together. He felt a boot nudge him in the ribs. He groaned and fought down the desire to retch.

'Get up.'

'You bastard. Untie me.'

'Can't do that, old sport. You've an important part to play in my plans.'

De Silva struggled feebly as Claybourne dragged him to his feet and hauled him to the nearest window. He was surprised to find the man was so strong.

'You're going to be my decoy,' Claybourne said coldly, producing another rope with which he tied de Silva to one of the bars. His stomach turned over. Why hadn't he foreseen this? The man was mad and he had walked straight into his trap. He should have brought Prasanna or Nadar with him, not just left a note saying where he had gone. But he mustn't show he was afraid.

'You're crazy if you think this will work, Claybourne. If it is Randall, he's bound to see I'm not you. He'll realise something's up and make a run for it.'

'If it was light and he could see you, I agree, but you know as well as I do that darkness falls quickly here. I told the guide to take a detour and make sure they arrive after sunset.'

He patted de Silva down and found the Webley. Removing it from its holster, he nodded. 'Reliable weapon this; better than mine. Good range too. I should be able to stop Randall with the first bullet.'

De Silva's blood roared in his ears. Suppose Claybourne wasn't as good a shot as he thought he was? If the man coming really was Randall and not Ralph, it was unlikely he would be unarmed. And even if Claybourne succeeds, he thought, where does that leave me? The answer stared him in the face: an inconvenient witness.

Claybourne pulled a roll of tape from his pocket and fixed a strip across de Silva's mouth. More tape trussed his ankles. Claybourne went back inside and emerged with a kerosene lamp which he hung from a beam. 'That should give Randall a bit of light but not enough to see your face. You and I are about the same height so that ought not to be a problem.'

The matter-of-fact tone filled de Silva with despair. Even if he had been able to talk, he doubted there was anything he could have said to change Claybourne's mind. He wanted vengeance for the wrong he believed had been done to his friend. Nothing was going to stand in his way. A suspicion crept into de Silva's mind that Claybourne's feelings for Wynne-Talbot might have gone beyond friendship.

Dusk quickly turned to darkness as they waited. At first, de Silva's arms throbbed then they became numb. The tape over his mouth made it impossible to take in air, but he forced himself to suppress the surges of panic he experienced and breathed steadily through his nose. He thought of Jane and faced the possibility he would never see her again. His heart ached at the prospect but he saw no way out.

A fatalistic calm settled on him as he listened to the sputter of the kerosene lamp and the sound of insects banging monotonously against its glass. The crescent moon threw a lurid light over the vista of ruined bushes and dry scrub. A breeze got up, rustling through the matted creepers that shrouded the old bungalow. He fancied he heard voices calling to him. Were they the voices of the dead?

A hiss from Claybourne's direction jolted him back to a state of full alertness. His heartbeat quickened. 'It's Randall,' Claybourne whispered. 'He's coming.'

For a few moments, two lights bobbed across the open ground then one of them curled away and was swallowed up by the jungle. It was impossible for de Silva's mouth to grow any dryer than it already was. He forgot to breathe through his nose and suffered another bout of panic that set his lungs on fire. Forcing himself to subdue it, he strained his eyes to make out the approaching figure's face. A few more paces and the man halted. 'Matthew?'

'Hello, Johnny.'

His captor's voice was so close it made de Silva start.

'I imagine you didn't expect to hear from me again,' Claybourne went on.

'So it's really you. But that's wonderful! It's marvellous to see you, old man. When I got your message, I hardly dared to believe it. Your name was on the casualty list. You were on it as missing, believed dead.'

'I wasn't far off. I spent three months in hospital with

severe burns and amnesia. The doctors told me afterwards that they hadn't expected me to pull through.'

'I can barely make you out there in the shadows. Move that lamp so we can see each other properly.'

'All in good time.'

'Why all this cloak-and-dagger stuff?' De Silva heard a note of uncertainty in Randall's jocular tone. 'We've a lot of catching up to do. Poor old Ralph – I expect you know he didn't make it. It was a dreadful shock for Helen.'

'Oh, but she had you to console her, didn't she?'

'Ah. That was a terrible mistake, Matthew. I've regretted it ever since. She led me on and I shouldn't have fallen for it. After the tragedy, the only honourable thing to do was stay with her. It's not been easy I can tell you.' His voice cracked. 'I expect you know how badly it's all ended.'

'Do you really think I'm gullible enough to believe you care for anyone but yourself?'

'I don't blame you for mistrusting me, Matthew.'

'And there's more, isn't there? You didn't just want Ralph's wife, you thought you'd have his life too.'

De Silva heard Randall's sharp intake of breath. For a moment, he seemed lost for an answer. In the silence, de Silva tried to make a noise to attract his attention but it was impossible. Then Randall rallied. 'I can explain—'

'I'm listening.'

'I realise some people would say what I'm doing's wrong, but look at it from my point of view. I wanted poor Helen to have the life that she would have had if Ralph hadn't died. I believe he really loved her at the end, so, if you like, it would expunge my guilt. His family are overjoyed. To them it's put right all the wrongs of the past. Let them keep that, Matthew.'

'Why did Helen die, Johnny? Did you drive her to it?'

'What the hell!'

'Don't act the innocent with me.'

'Of course I didn't. It was an accident. I would never have hurt her. I was determined to care for her for Ralph's sake. You and he were the best friends I ever had.'

An edge came into Claybourne's voice. 'A strange way to treat a friend, Johnny.'

'Helen started it, Matthew. If she hadn't given me the eye—'

'Don't keep blaming it all on her.'

'I'm sorry. I admit I was at fault too.' He groaned. 'God, what a bloody disaster it's all been. I'd do anything to be able to go back and put it all right.'

De Silva squirmed and tried to move. The feeling had gone from his arms and his chest ached but he shifted his head forward and back enough to bang it against the bars. The inside of his skull jangled with the impact and he didn't try again. The sound was muffled, but Randall must have heard it. 'What's that?' he asked sharply.

'Rats, I expect. The place is riddled with them.'

To de Silva's despair, Randall seemed satisfied.

'Come on, Matthew. We can't bring Ralph and Helen back to life but we can still be friends.'

'Can we?' Bitterness infused Claybourne's voice. 'I saw you do it, Johnny.'

'What do you mean?'

'I saw you kill Ralph. You didn't realise I was lying nearby, did you? I saw what you did.'

'Matthew, you can't think…'

'No?'

'He was in agony, Matthew. Almost gone. He begged me to put him out of his misery.'

The first bullet passed close to de Silva's ear. Its heat seared his skin. The sound was so loud that it deafened him for a moment.

Claybourne's aim must have been wide of the mark. Randall didn't stumble or cry out. Metal glinted in the darkness. De Silva braced himself as Randall fired in return, but that bullet also went wide, burying itself in the wall. The noise still reverberated when the third shot rang out. This time, Randall reeled and fell to the ground. De Silva's bones turned to water and he closed his eyes.

When he opened them, Claybourne knelt by Randall. After a few moments, he hauled himself to his feet. 'He's dead,' he said flatly, as he looked down at the body. He stepped away and the barrel of his gun caught the light.

De Silva held his breath. Did he want to face the bullet that would end his life, or let it come out of darkness? He chose the first; he wouldn't be a coward at the end. Willing a goodbye to Jane that she would never hear, he held his breath. He thought his heart would explode from his chest as the black circle followed an upward curve. His knees sagged and horror engulfed him. The gun rose higher until it reached Claybourne's right temple. And there it stopped.

* * *

Something scrabbled over his body, rousing him from his stupefied state. The kerosene lamp had gone out but the moon was high. By its light, he saw a creature he identified as a langur monkey. It sprang away as he moved and went to perch on Matthew Claybourne's lifeless body. Its jaws worked as if it was making the angry, high-pitched screeching noise langurs emitted when they were alarmed, but the sound was strangely dim. His ears throbbed.

His inclination was to close his eyes again and slip into unconsciousness but he forced himself not to. Moistening his lips with his tongue, he found that the tape had loosened enough for him to suck it in. With a little more effort, he nipped it between his front teeth; more persistence and he had made a gash in it. He leant forward and gulped a deep breath of pure night air.

The monkey leapt off Claybourne's body and bounded away into the bungalow. Left alone on the verandah, de Silva spent the next hour working his ankles free. His hands were a harder challenge; the rope had hardly any give in it. Even after another hour of twisting and turning, he had only loosened his bonds a fraction.

Cramp and the pain where the rope abraded his skin were excruciating and the throbbing in his ears had intensified to a burning sensation. He rested for a few minutes then changed his tactics. Bending one knee, he put his foot flat against the wall and pushed hard while throwing his weight forward with all the force he could muster. After three attempts, he moved to the other leg. He had almost given up hope when the bar shifted a little.

It gave him the confidence to redouble his efforts until at last it gave way, catapulting him to the floor. He lay winded for a while, deciding what to do, then he remembered the plate with the remains of Claybourne's meal. He was sure there had been a knife there. If he could get to it, it might be possible to use it in some way to cut through the rope.

Gritting his teeth, he staggered to his feet and shook the broken bar free of the rope. It clattered to the ground and he froze as he saw a flicker of movement in the darkness beyond the kerosene lamplight. Claybourne still lay motionless but what if he had been wrong and Johnny Randall wasn't dead? The fellow would be crazy to let a witness live. His heart thudded and he froze then a black shape swooped from the eaves and soared into the darkness. A bat. Gradually, his heartbeat steadied.

Inside the bungalow, it was very dark and it took him several minutes to find the table. Laying his cheek on the surface, he felt around for the plate and knife but they were gone. He cursed then remembered the monkey. It must have come for the food. Maybe it had knocked the plate on the floor.

After another painstaking search he found it. He made a shuffling turn and managed to locate the knife. The floor was made of wooden boards, roughly laid. If he could nudge the knife over to one of the gaps and wedge the blade in, it might hold steady enough to enable him to cut through the rope around his wrists.

It was a slow process and more than once he had to stop to stretch and roll his shoulders in an attempt to ease the stiffness and pain that by now plagued his bruised and battered body. At last, the section of rope he was working on split. His strength failing, he pulled his wrists free.

The relief was overwhelming. He stumbled to his feet and tottered into the other room then collapsed on the low bed. It smelt of mildew but he didn't care. At that moment, he wouldn't have changed it for a room at the Crown Hotel.

His eyes closed, and he slept.

CHAPTER 30

Hebden unwound the bandages around de Silva's wrists and carefully inspected the still-angry wounds.

'Hmm.' He dabbed away some pus with a piece of cotton wool soaked in surgical spirit and de Silva flinched. Hebden looked up. 'Sorry. I'd like to keep these covered for a few more days. I'll re-bandage them for you.'

'Thank you.'

'How's the head?'

'The headache has gone.'

'Still got a bit of ringing in the ears though?'

'Yes.'

'That should pass. As you were so close, the impact of the gunshots will have affected your ears. It's not uncommon to suffer some discomfort and loss of hearing for a while. You were lucky though. It could so easily have been much worse.'

De Silva nodded. He was well aware that his brush with death had been close, and, if he hadn't been, the dismayed telling-off Jane gave him when she found out about the episode would have left him in no doubt.

'I'd like to get back to work on Monday,' he said resolutely when Hebden had brought scissors and lint from his bag and got to work.

'No doubt, but I don't advise it. I'll come again in a couple of days and we'll talk about it then.' He neatened the second bandage then replaced the scissors and the remaining lint in his bag. 'In any event, I don't think it would be wise to arouse your wife's ire at the moment.'

De Silva grinned sheepishly. 'Probably not.'

'By the way, I thought you might be interested in some information uncovered when Randall's possessions were searched. Archie Clutterbuck decided he ought to try and find out if there was anyone who should be notified of his death but there was no indication of it.'

'But?'

'He did find a stock of pills in Randall's baggage – Nembutal. The very thing that Randall asked me for and I turned him down. There's no one else he could have consulted this side of Kandy so I deduce that he brought them with him when he came to Nuala. If he already had his wife taking them, I believe that would have made her fragile state worse. If I'm right, even though he didn't kill her, he hastened her death.'

'But why didn't he dispose of them?'

'No time? Or he wanted to do it when he was far away from Nuala and there was no danger of anyone spotting them?'

'Perhaps you're right.'

Hebden closed the clasp of his bag with a snap. 'Well, I must be on my way. Other patients to see.' He put a restraining hand on de Silva's shoulder. 'No, don't try to get up. Your balance will have been impaired too, and although I'm confident it will right itself with a few more days' rest, you must be patient.'

He picked up his bag and went to the top of the verandah steps, stopping there for a moment to survey the garden. 'Your roses look very fine,' he remarked. 'Content yourself with enjoying them. Plenty of time for other things when you're fully recovered.'

Left alone, de Silva sighed and reached for the copy of

Pride and Prejudice on the table beside him. He found his place and did his best to pay attention to the story but his mind wandered. A peacock flew down from a tree, disturbing the stillness that the heat had imposed on the garden. He watched it fan its iridescent tail feathers in the sun then strut and peck for insects in the grass. Such a magnificent bird with its gorgeous plumage, its splendour enhanced by the haughty air of an aloof society beauty.

Jane found him dozing when she returned from a visit an hour later. He roused himself quickly. 'I wasn't asleep. Only resting my eyes.'

'Of course you were. Have you had a pleasant morning?'

'I've not done much. Hebden came then I read for a while.'

'What did he say?'

'He told me to rest and keep the bandages on for a few more days.'

'Quite right too. Everyone has been very concerned about you, you know.'

He grimaced. 'I'm not sure Clutterbuck or William Petrie were too pleased with the turn things took. They might have preferred it if Randall had been a better shot.'

'Shanti!'

'Well, he would have removed an inconvenient witness to the truth and no one would have been any the wiser.'

'I'm sure that's the last thing they would have wanted.'

'That's because it would never occur to you that it might be a good thing, my love.'

Jane clicked her tongue. 'If you're going to start feeling sorry for yourself, I refuse to listen to another word.' She patted his shoulder. 'Seriously, you mustn't be disconsolate, dear. You did the right thing. They ought to respect that, even though it may take a little while for them to come round.'

'It's not only that. I am unhappy to have been the one

to bring sadness into Lady Caroline's life. She is a lady I admire and to have her joy at being reunited with her nephew shattered in such a cruel way—'

'But what Randall did wasn't your fault, dear.'

'I know, but…'

She bent down and kissed his cheek. 'I do understand, but I'm sure she'll recover. And she's a good woman. I very much doubt she would want Randall to benefit from his crime.'

'I hope you're right.'

'Now, it's nearly time for lunch. Cook has made all your favourites. That should cheer you up.'

* * *

'I forgot to mention that Sergeant Prasanna is coming this afternoon,' said Jane as they drank coffee on the verandah after their meal. 'I expect you would like to thank him.'

De Silva nodded. He hadn't had a chance to speak to Prasanna yet and would be glad to. In his weakened and confused state, his plight at the coffee plantation would have been dire indeed had it not been for his sergeant.

It was Prasanna who had read the note de Silva had taken the precaution of leaving on his desk and who had gone to the guest house early the following morning. He had questioned the owner and, from the information he obtained, traced the guide who had brought Randall to the plantation. The man had taken some persuading, including the exchange of money, but he had eventually agreed to lead Prasanna to the scene of the crime.

'I assume that he isn't just coming to enquire after my health?' he asked with a smile.

Jane chuckled. 'Yes, he does have another motive.' She lowered her voice. 'His mother has asked him to bring Kuveni to tea.'

'Goodness me, this is progress.'

'Yes, it certainly is.'

She finished her coffee and put down her cup. 'I have a few letters to write. Florence asked me to help her on the committee for her next charity event. Will you be alright here for a while?'

'Of course. I can read some more of my book. Or maybe as Doctor Hebden advises, I should simply admire the roses.'

'What a sensible idea. I must say, the more I know of Doctor Hebden, the more I like him.'

Jane hadn't been gone long and he only had a few pages left to read when one of the servants appeared in the doorway. 'Sergeant Prasanna is here, sahib. Shall I show him in?'

'Please do.'

Even though it was a Saturday, the sergeant was in uniform. His dark, unruly hair was neatly slicked back and a passing beetle could have seen itself in the toes of his shoes.

'Good afternoon, sir. I hope you are feeling better?'

'I am, and I owe you a debt of thanks. You did an excellent job of finding me.'

Prasanna beamed. 'Thank you, sir.'

They chatted for a while. De Silva was pleased to hear that nothing had unduly troubled the calm at the police station while he had been away. 'So,' he said after a few minutes. 'I understand from my wife that you and Miss Kuveni have an engagement this afternoon.'

'Yes, sir.' A little of the confidence in Prasanna's voice ebbed then he rallied. 'My mother has asked me to bring her to our home.'

'And I'm sure the occasion will go like a ticking clock.' De Silva smiled encouragingly.

'I hope you're right, sir.'

'Of course I am. Well, you'd better be on your way. Go inside and find one of the servants. They'll know where

Kuveni is. Thank you again for all you did, and for coming to visit me. Doctor Hebden and Mrs de Silva are in league to keep me here for a few more days but I'll be back at the station as soon as I manage to escape their clutches.'

'That is good news, sir.'

Ah, thought de Silva with a sigh, as the young man hurried off, how fortunate Prasanna was to be young and fit. Just now, de Silva felt battered and very old. He reached once more for his book. Doubtless, Miss Austen would have shared Jane's robust views on self-pity, so he had better not indulge in it.

The sound of the book sliding from his lap jerked him awake and, at the same moment, the telephone rang in the hall. His ears must be improving. He probably wouldn't have heard it a few days ago. Jane must have been close to it for the ringing stopped and he heard her voice speaking to the caller. A few moments later, she came out to the verandah.

'How nice,' she said brightly. 'That was Joan Buscott. They are leaving for England early next week and she wants to come and say goodbye. I've invited her to have some tea with us.'

'I'm not sure—'

'Oh, won't you at least say hello to her? I don't expect she'll stay long and she's so kind. She told me she was most concerned about you.'

De Silva felt guilty. From what he knew of Joan Buscott, she was a very pleasant and kindly lady. He nodded. 'I'm sorry. It's just rather sudden.'

'If you get tired and want to rest, I'm sure she won't be offended.'

An hour later, just as the clock on the drawing room mantelpiece struck half past four, they heard the sound of a car crunching over the gravel. The front doorbell shrilled, followed shortly afterwards by the murmur of voices. Jane got up to go and greet the visitor.

When she returned, de Silva lurched forward in his chair in surprise. He had expected to see Joan Buscott's homely, smiling face under its tidy pleat of grey hair, but not the elegant woman dressed in a pale-grey ensemble who accompanied her. Unsteadily, he hauled himself to his feet.

'Lady Caroline!'

'Oh, please sit down, Inspector. There's really no need for ceremony.'

'I am honoured,' he said lamely. If only there had been more notice of her visit, he might have felt more composed.

'Joan and I are old friends,' said Lady Caroline briskly when they had all sat down. 'So when I told her I wished to see you, she suggested I accompany her today. Inspector, I'll get to the point. I want to assure you that you did the right thing. It was a terrible shock to me at first but that has now passed.' She gave a sad smile. 'My family didn't always obtain their lands and privileges by praiseworthy means but they have always been of the blood and I believe that should not change. The death of my poor nephew was tragic but it must be accepted. The prospect of a rogue like Randall taking his place is abhorrent.'

A wistful expression came over her face. 'It's a small consolation to me that my father never found out about any of this. The title and estate will go to a cousin of mine who is the next heir. As a boy, he often stayed at Axford and my father was fond of him. He'll be a worthy successor.'

De Silva's mind reeled. It seemed that providence had decided to favour him. He felt his shoulders go down.

'My husband has been obliged to return to Kandy,' Lady Caroline went on, 'but he asked me to send his good wishes for your speedy recovery. He also asked me to tell you that he is recommending you for a commendation for your bravery.'

'Please thank him, my lady. His kindness is more than I deserve.'

Lady Caroline smiled. 'There I have to disagree with you, Inspector.'

The rest of the conversation flowed easily over the clink of teacups. De Silva found that his appetite for the savouries and butter cake Cook had managed to produce at such short notice had improved remarkably. On further thought, he wondered if the visit was not as impromptu as Jane had liked to make out.

When the visitors had left, he leant back in his chair, relief lightening his heart. Jane's instincts were usually reliable. If William Petrie was on his side, Archie Clutterbuck would surely come round. But best of all, Lady Caroline forgave him.

Dusk softened the outlines of the garden; the humid air throbbed with cicadas as the sun sank with the swiftness of the tropics. He smiled to himself. This teatime diplomacy was clearly an excellent thing. Perhaps if there was more of it, the world would be a better place.

The dark shapes of a flock of egrets going to their roost arrowed across the sky. Soon, Jane would come to call him inside, but he wanted to watch a little longer. Peace had returned to Sunnybank.

CHAPTER 31

Two months later

Jane looked up from the new film magazine she was glancing at over breakfast. 'Gracious, how interesting.'

'What's that?' De Silva put down the *Colombo Times* he had been reading.

'Laetitia Lane and Major Aubrey.'

'Oh?'

'They're in Hollywood.'

De Silva's forehead wrinkled. 'In America?'

'Is there another place called Hollywood?'

'Probably not. What does it say about them?'

'I'll read it to you. *This week Hollywood welcomes Miss Laetitia Lane, star of London's West End stage. Miss Lane arrived in style on the Queen Mary. She is contracted to Mammoth Productions to make three motion pictures. Her manager, Mr Aubrey St James* – but it's definitely Major Aubrey; there's a photograph of them both – *who accompanies her said Miss Lane was delighted to be in America. It's been her lifelong ambition to see our great country. More pictures on page...* etcetera, etcetera. Well! I always thought Laetitia Lane wouldn't be kept down for long. I wonder what the two of them are really up to in America.'

'More than meets the eye maybe. I doubt we'll ever know.'

'Will you be coming home for lunch today, dear?'

De Silva scooped up the last of the string hoppers on his plate and wiped his mouth with his napkin. 'I intended to, will you be in?'

'No, Kuveni and I are going to town to see about ordering her wedding sari. You don't mind, do you? I want her to have something special. Her father and brother have offered what they can afford and, if you remember, we talked about making up the rest.'

'Of course I don't mind.'

'And we're meeting Sergeant Prasanna's mother, so I'll leave instructions with Cook to have something ready for you.'

'Thank you.' He grinned. 'I wish you a successful trip. I hope Mrs Prasanna won't try to take charge too much.'

Jane sniffed. 'Oh, I think Kuveni and I can handle Mrs Prasanna. She's really a very nice woman when one gets to know her. She's very keen to help with the preparations for the wedding too. Kuveni may not have been the daughter-in-law she had in mind, but she seems to have accepted the situation. Better than losing her son, and luckily she and Kuveni already get on rather well.'

'Good. That must be a weight off Prasanna's mind.'

'I'm sure it is, and I doubt many people will dare risk his mother's wrath by criticising his choice.' She sighed. 'But glad as I am that everything has turned out for the best, I'll miss Kuveni.'

He gave her a sympathetic smile. 'I will too,' he said and meant it. With her kind heart and graceful charm, the girl had brought sunshine into the house. It had been a taste of what might have been... But no, he wouldn't dwell on that.

'Let's hope she visits us often,' he said briskly. 'Now, I should be on my way. Enjoy your shopping trip. Don't come back too tired out. I have a plan for this evening.'

Jane gave him a puzzled frown. 'I don't think there's

anything on at the Casino or a band at the dance hall. What do you have in mind?'

He stood up and tapped the side of his nose. 'You'll have to wait and see. It's a surprise.'

At the station, he went into his office and hauled out the large, unwieldy box that sat on the floor of the big store cupboard. It had arrived from England only yesterday, too late for their anniversary unfortunately, but it could be an extra gift.

How convenient that Jane would be out today. Slitting the tapes that bound it, he lifted the flaps and peered inside. It didn't look too complicated and fortunately there were some instructions. He'd take it home at the end of the morning and set it up in the room next to the dining room. There was very little furniture there and they rarely used it.

Later, at Sunnybank, a servant hurried out to help as he manhandled the box out of the Morris's passenger seat. When they had carried it to the room and set it down on the low chest by the window, he took out his handkerchief and mopped his brow. Even though the ill effects of his encounter with Claybourne and Randall had, thankfully, worn off, he wasn't as fit as he would like to be. Still, perhaps this box held the answer.

'Not a word of this to your mistress,' he told the servant. 'It's to be a surprise.'

'Yes, master.'

De Silva pulled back the flaps of the box and took out the brass horn then he and the servant lifted out the mahogany box containing the mechanism and the turntable. Before long, the gramophone was wound up and ready to test out. He removed the case containing the records he had ordered from its separate compartment in the box, chose one and put it on the turntable. The servant's eyes widened as music emerged from the brass horn. They listened for a few moments then de Silva removed the needle and closed the lid. He gestured to the table and chairs. 'All we need to do now is move these back to the wall to make space in the middle of the room.'

A bit of huffing and puffing and it was done. 'Excellent,' said de Silva. 'All ready to go. But remember – not a word.'

As he ate a solitary lunch on the verandah, he thought of the records he'd chosen. Love: it was the theme of most songs. Love in all its many guises. Where would songwriters be without it? Indeed, where would the human race be? Songs, novels, films – to say nothing of the real thing. There was love that brought reconciliation like Prasanna and Kuveni's; doomed love like Matthew Claybourne's and Ralph Wynne-Talbot's; destructive love like the tragic Helen's, and selfish love like Johnny Randall's – a close cousin of greed and egotism that left a bitter legacy. Then there was the quiet, undramatic kind of love, the kind that acted as the bedrock of so many lives: the love between parents and children, and between husbands and wives.

Lunch eaten, he sat and drank his coffee, watching a pair of bee-eaters flit about in the branches of the tulip tree nearby. The one he assumed was the male from the extra brightness of its green and blue plumage paused on a branch to sing, its dark eyes sharp and its orange bib swelling with the effort of the performance. Love again – even birds and animals weren't immune to it.

There was nothing urgent waiting for him at the station. A good day to take the afternoon off. He'd finished his latest book and he wasn't in the mood for starting a new one. The female bee-eater flew away, pursued by the male. The garden drowsed in the heat. Perhaps he'd do the same.

* * *

'Shanti?'

He woke with a start to see Jane standing in the doorway, a teasing smile on her face.

'What time is it?'

'Nearly four. I guessed I might find you here. You'll be rivalling Constable Nadar soon.'

'Just resting my eyes. How did the shopping trip go?'

'Very well. We've chosen some beautiful silk for the sari. Kuveni will look a picture.'

'Has she come back with you?'

'No, she's stayed in town. Prasanna's mother insisted they both have a meal with her so Prasanna will bring her home in a rickshaw later. She asked if I would stay but I said I needed to get back to you. It's a family occasion and I didn't want to impose. Anyway, I'm dying to know what this surprise is.'

He got up. 'I'll satisfy your curiosity but you must close your eyes first.'

Jane's brow wrinkled. 'You're being very mysterious. What's this all about?'

'You'll soon find out. Give me your hand.'

He led her to the room beside the dining room and opened the door.

'Can I look yet?'

'Just a moment longer.' He let go of her hand. 'Stay there and don't move.'

He crossed to the gramophone and lifted the lid then pulled the arm back gently until it clicked and the turntable started to revolve. He placed the needle in the groove of the record and took a breath. 'You can open your eyes now.'

Jane clapped her hands. 'A gramophone! What a lovely surprise. How did you know I wanted one?'

'I guessed. Now we can dance whenever we like.'

She laughed. 'Shanti, dear, it's only teatime, and I'm not dressed for dancing.'

'What does that matter?'

The sound of the strings, woodwind and brass of the BBC Dance Orchestra, under the baton of Henry Hall, filled the room.

'Shall we?'

'With pleasure, kind sir.' She stepped into his arms.

As the music swelled, he spun her round.

'Shanti, not so fast! You'll make me giddy! And you must count. We're out of time.'

'But I am counting. It's just the music that is too slow.'

Jane rolled her eyes. 'And mind the furniture.'

'The furniture is perfectly safe and now who is not concentrating?' He pulled her closer and they both started to laugh as Les Allen began to croon.

Love is the Sweetest Thing...

He couldn't have put it better himself.